Rogan
Fated Dragon Daddies
Book 5

Pepper North

Pepper North
With a Wink Publishing, LLC

Text copyright© 2025 Pepper North®
All Rights Reserved

Pepper North® is a registered trademark.
All rights reserved.

NO AI TRAINING: Without in any way limiting the author's [and publisher's] exclusive rights under copyright, any use of this publication to "train" generative artificial intelligence (AI) technologies to generate text is expressly prohibited. The author reserves all rights to license uses of this work for generative AI training and development of machine learning language models.

Author's Note:

The following story is completely fictional. The characters are all over the age of 18 and as adults choose to live their lives in an age play environment.

This is a series of books that can be read in any order. You may, however, choose to read them sequentially to enjoy the characters best. Subsequent books will feature characters that appear in previous novels as well as new faces.

You can contact me on
my Pepper North Facebook pages,
at www.4peppernorth.club
eMail at 4peppernorth@gmail.com
I'm experimenting with Instagram, Twitter, and Tiktok.
Come join me everywhere!

Prologue

Nestled in the center of a ring of imposing mountains, the village of Wyvern has existed for hundreds of years. Its quaint town center wraps around a square featuring a commanding dragon statue elevated on a block-wide platform for all to admire. The words chiseled into the risers of the stone steps are a mystery to most. Almost all the ninety-plus commemorative etchings feature the last names of the founding families of the town without explanation. During the prosperity of technological tools, most forgot the old ways.

One female descendant of each founding family has traditionally served as the keeper of knowledge. Passing a huge tome from generation to generation, that woman ensures the pact the original settlers made with the first inhabitants of this land can't be forgotten. The agreement between the huge, lethal creatures living in the mountaintops and the struggling, besieged humans sealed the duties for both sides. Promising protection for the people and fated mates for the dragons, this pact has evaporated from the minds of most of the citizens of Wyvern. But the dragons have not forgotten.

When all things powered by technology suddenly ceased to

function, the worst features of humanity erupted as people struggled to survive. Once again, the strength and power of the massive beasts who have guarded the city is needed. Revealing themselves to the current-day citizens, the dragon horde fulfills their promise.

As descendants of those original families are found, mate bonds are forged between dragons and humans. The old ways are essential to the survival of all, and the ancient pact will soar in importance once again. For there are dragons, and they hunt for more than just prey.

Five dragons of the horde have recently discovered their mates in the growing population of Wyvern. Others still search, hoping that each day brings their mate back to their ancestors' home. The stakes are dire for the shifters. Mates create a balance between their human and dragon identities. One teeters on the brink of madness without the companionship of a mate.

Chapter 1

Brooks had discovered that communal gatherings had become the norm in Wyvern these days. Sheltered together from the craziness he'd experienced himself outside the protective mountain ring around the ancient city, the Wyverns had grown closer as they had to rely on each other to survive. These town-wide celebrations were a uniting break from hard labor.

He glanced around, looking for people he recognized. A drawback from being away for so long was that he struggled to match the young friends from his memory with the older faces around him. When he caught sight of Skye, he headed her way. He'd like to make sure she was as happy as she appeared. After spending time with the unique woman, he cared about her. The group of mates appeared to accept her completely. Here was his chance to see for himself.

"Hey, Skye. Can I join you?"

He smiled at the four mates and their dragon shifters as they glanced up. To his delight, Skye nodded enthusiastically and patted the ground near her.

"Brooks, I'm glad you're here," Lalani greeted him. She was

a familiar face as well. His grandmother loved the dragon's mate and met with her often.

Settling between the two women, Brooks caught up with the latest news. Skye, as usual, didn't say much. He was tickled when she cared enough to ask him anything.

"You're staying in Wyvern?"

"It's safe here. There's a lot to do, so I can keep busy. I've been working on the passageways under the old town. I'm feeling like a tunnel rat. My grandmother insisted I come today to interact with people," Brooks shared before shaking his head and adding, "I hate to say, I'm getting itchy to travel. I'm not used to hanging around the same place."

"Your grandmother is so happy to have you here," Lalani said.

"I know. I'm not climbing the walls yet. Just trying to decide what to do long-term," Brooks assured her.

Skye patted Brooks on the shoulder. Immediately, two warning growls made him freeze and raise his hands to show he was harmless. Ardon and Oldrik were obviously protective of their mate. The blue dragon claimed Skye, placing her on his lap.

Brooks chose the wisest move when dealing with a jealous dragon. He excused himself and shifted to the other side of Lalani. Keeping his eye on Skye, he suspected Skye and her mates were talking mentally. She seemed thrilled with her mates. Brooks was pleased for her.

Like something that special would ever happen for me.

A tune Skye hummed under her breath sparked interest as almost everyone recognized it. Brooks had always called it the "Ode to Wyvern." It was a song all Wyverns learned as a child. Ciel began to sing, and the other mates joined her, including the dragons. Suddenly the words took on true meaning. Chills went down Brooks's spine.

Wyvern. Oh, Wyvern, we reached you in a battered state.
Will your mountain barriers guard us from those who hate?
Seeking sanctuary, the families dared to make a deal.
Winged creatures and Guardians allowed us to heal.
All hail those who are selected!
All hail those whose fate is sealed!
Engrave their names in stone for all to celebrate.
Never ever forget the ones predestined as mate,
For the fiery beasts, while fierce, are honor bound.
Each match creates Wyvern's protected ground.
All hail those who are selected!
All hail those whose fate is sealed!

"It's about us. About those fated to join with dragons." Tears filled Aurora's eyes.

"I've heard that a thousand times and never stopped to understand the meaning of the lines." Ciel shook her head in disbelief.

Wringing her hands, Lalani requested, "Teach it to me. I want to memorize this as well."

She'd missed learning this from her birth family.

Of course, the other mates sang it with Lalani until she was confident she'd remember it. The chills remained as they rehearsed the tune. Finally, Lalani requested to try it on her own. Her beautiful alto voice was hesitant at first but gained strength and confidence.

He held his breath as Skye sang with her. The combination of the two was magical. Time seemed to stop in its tracks. When the last note faded away, a large man walked toward the gathered group, clapping his powerful hands together. The new arrival's piercing blue eyes and chiseled body captured Brooks's attention in a way Brooks didn't understand. Confused by his reaction, Brooks sat up straight.

"How many freaking dragon shifters are there?" Brooks wondered. That had to be a dragon. He was massive.

Politely, the crowd joined in his applause. Brooks suddenly didn't care about anyone else. Something kept him focused on the dragon. He was magnetic, simply standing there. Why on earth did Brooks have the urge to touch him? Brooks lost track of everything going on when the dragon lifted his nose to capture a scent in the air.

Unable to stop himself, Brooks rose to his feet. The dragon shifter concentrated his entire attention on Brooks, who stiffened his spine and forced himself not to move, not understanding what was happening to him.

Come. I am Rogan. And you are temptation incarnate.

Brooks's feet moved as if by their own accord toward the shifter. When he paused in front of the magnetic dragon, Brooks couldn't resist lifting his fingers to brush away the red lock of hair that had fallen over the newcomer's forehead. An audible sizzle and a burning pain on the back of his hand didn't distract Brooks from the triumphant gleam in the shifter's eyes.

"Mine."

Exhausting all his willpower, Brooks jerked his gaze away from the dragon's. He checked out his hand. The skin was vaguely red, but the shape hadn't formed yet. He knew it would. Brooks had lived with his grandmother and her stories of the history of Wyvern for too many years before setting off to find adventure.

"The Battlefield family. I was not aware they had a potential mate," Rogan stated before suggesting, "We appear to be the center of attention. May I take you somewhere private where we can talk?"

"Brooks?"

Pulling his attention away from Rogan, Brooks focused on his grandmother's proud face. "Hi, Grandma. This is Rogan."

"I have met the red dragon many times. He is very honorable. The Battlefield family is honored to provide you with a mate, Rogan." Eleonore recited the traditional words of the founding family's guardian.

Brooks struggled to process all of this. He knew there were male mates but had never dreamed he would be one. His world had suddenly flipped upside down.

"My thanks to the Battlefield clan. I will guard and protect not only Wyvern and your family, but my treasured mate for all his life," Rogan responded, power and commitment ringing from his words.

Brooks couldn't decide whether to panic or celebrate. He remained locked in place, waiting to see what would happen.

Rogan turned to press his hand to the small of Brooks's back. Brooks stifled a moan of delight as the impact of Rogan's touch struck him. He'd never experienced anything like the sensation of complete rightness blended with sexual heat. Brooks struggled to control his body's reaction. His cock twitched in his pants threatening to reveal the instant desire Rogan created inside him.

Our connection is strong, Mate. I will help.

Brooks's shoulders relaxed into place as something like a blanket settled over the fire growing inside it. It didn't smother it. That sensual attraction still simmered but at a level he could handle in public.

Shaking his head in amazement and relief, Brooks met Rogan's gaze. *Thank you.* He waited to see the dragon's reaction.

Rogan shook his head. *I can't hear you yet, Brooks. Soon, our connection will be stronger. I will fly us to a neutral spot a distance from the crowd so we can talk.*

Brooks glanced over his shoulder at the mates behind him who chattered happily as they watched how he and Rogan interacted. Was he part of them now? Brooks needed to figure out this connection away from observers. "Let's go."

"I will step away and change. Stay close. The bond will remain tight between us."

In a few seconds, Brooks stood next to a freaking dragon. Sure, Keres, the black dragon, had carried him in his claws. That, he never wished to repeat. He'd screamed inside a million times as Keres had swooped through the skies. If the dragon had relaxed his hold for a split second, Brooks would have tumbled to an excruciating death.

At that thought, he retreated a few feet, only to be speared with a jolt of agony that shook Brooks to the core. His eyes closed as he dropped to a fetal position to protect himself. *What the hell?* The ground rumbled below his feet as the pain disappeared.

Mate. Our bond is tight. Are you okay?

Brooks forced himself to open his eyes and had to plant his feet not to retreat again. Gorgeous red eyes the size of platters were inches from him. The discomfort receded when the dragon stood close. What would such a glorious beast feel like? He scrambled to his feet.

Curious, he reached out to run his hand over the dragon's scales. Rogan closed his eyes in delight. The obvious delight from his touch helped Brooks's heart to stop pounding so desperately. Brooks dared to stroke the beast's jawline and heard what sounded like a rumble inside his skull.

"You purr?"

Of course not. Ask me something with your mind.

You purr?

Still a no on the purr thing. However, I hear you clearly now. Are you ready to go for a ride?

You won't let go? Brooks wanted, no needed, to check.

Let go?

Rogan

Keres flew me, Skye, and Derek to town.

A blast of anger made Brooks flinch.

My apologies, Mate. Keres did not know you were a mate. He would have treated you with greater care if he had.

A shadow passed over them, making man and beast look up. The black dragon landed a distance from them and dipped his wings before shifting to go talk to the others. He did not approach them.

Climb up on my shoulders, Brooks. Hold on to my neck. Rogan bent his front leg to provide a step for Brooks.

Unsure how to not hurt the dragon, Brooks hesitantly followed his directions. He must have been thinking too hard about being careful, for laughter sounded in his brain.

You are precious, Mate. I can survive direct blasts of fire. You will not damage my scales.

You're eavesdropping. I'm sure you'd rather I be cautious than rip scales out. Brooks didn't enjoy being the source of amusement for the dragon. He was already completely off-balance. Brooks didn't need to be a joke as well.

My apologies, Brooks. I didn't mean to offend you. You're enchanting. I appreciate your wish to care for me. I feel the same way.

Made it, Brooks announced as he settled into place. He wrapped his arms around the dragon's neck. Power coursed through the creature's form, and close up, the shiny black scales held a myriad of colors within them. Surprised by his appreciation of the dragon's handsomeness, Brooks guarded his private thoughts from Rogan. *I'm ready.*

Then we go.

The dragon's bulk below him tensed, and the massive creature launched into the air. Brooks tightened his arms and pressed his face to the side of the dragon's neck to lessen the wind whipping around him. When Brooks dared to open his eyes, the view astonished him. Sitting here was a stark contrast from Brooks's previous experience dangling within the claws of the black dragon.

Warm reassurance emanated from the dragon, calming Brooks's nerves and smoothing out the fear he remembered. This was awesome. As they passed over the city center, he noticed all the people waving. The dragons had helped so much since the loss of technology. The citizens now honored them with their eager greetings and sought their aid and protection just as they had when the pact was created.

Scanning the ring of mountains in front of him, Brooks asked, *Which peak is yours?*

The red one, of course. I will land at the base, and we can talk.

A roar sounded behind them. Brooks turned together with the dragon to spot what came up behind them. A huge black beast powered by thunderous flaps of his wings. Keres.

Hold on tight, Brooks. Change of plans.

He didn't have to tell Brooks twice. Something in the dragon's call alerted him that Keres was dangerous. Combining that with the stress he sensed in Rogan's tone made him hang on to his mate. Hopefully, he wasn't strangling Rogan as the dragon increased his speed and altitude. They raced through the air toward the top of the mountain before them. Brooks could see a faint redness of the exposed soil in scattered spots. It loomed ahead of them.

An abrupt roll to the left caught Brooks by surprise, and he clung to Rogan. A blast of pure heat flamed by where they had just been. Brooks's heartrate quickened. Keres wasn't playing. Rogan didn't return the attack. Brooks knew without him the dragon would have met Keres straight on. He was a liability.

Never! Hold on. I have a secret.

Brooks didn't think he could plaster himself closer, but he

tried. A wall of water loomed in front of them. Rogan flew straight toward the cascade and the rocks. The dragon's nose disappeared into the stream. Shaking with fear, Brooks took a quick breath as the water swallowed Rogan's massive skull. The deluge over his head made him close his eyes.

Then a wave of heat rolled over his skin. Brooks's eyelids flipped open. Rogan flew through an open circle of flame. Instinctively checking behind him, he watched the fiery entrance narrow to hug the dragon's scales after Brooks passed through. The dragon's muscles bunched as he put on the brakes. Brooks whirled around to spot a solid slab of stone loom in front of them. There wasn't time to scream. Figuring this was it, Brooks hid his face in the dragon's scales.

Brooks. You're safe. Keres can't reach us here.

Brooks forced his hands to relax before sitting up. "I'm never flying on a dragon again."

He was done.

Chapter 2

Slide down, Brooks. I need to hold you.

Only following those directions because standing on solid ground was his greatest desire, Brooks negotiated his way off the dragon. His knees shook in reaction to the arrival. Brooks leaned forward to brace his hands on his thighs as he took deep breaths.

The air swirled around him before warm arms wrapped around his torso, drawing him upright before hugging him close. Not used to being weak, Brooks struggled to get away, but Rogan squeezed him tightly to his hard form. Inside, Brooks wanted to let Rogan support him, but worried what Rogan would think.

"Relax, Brooks. It's okay to be vulnerable with me. No one is watching."

"That dragon is an asshole. You should all torch him."

"He is unstable. Keres flirts with madness without a mate. He and I were the last two unmated dragons in our horde."

"And you found me?"

"And I found you," Rogan confirmed. "He was okay until

he wasn't. The horde will have to make a tough decision soon. But not today."

Rogan brushed away the bangs that had flopped over Brooks's eyes. "I was not expecting you, Mate." He wrapped his hand around the back of Brooks's head and drew him closer.

Brooks held his breath. An overwhelming attraction filled him, but this was way outside his experience. Rogan's lips met his softly once before he slammed down on his mouth. The man and shifter battled for dominance. Aggressive kisses ignited the bond between them.

Rogan's hands stroked over Brooks. The dragon's barely controlled strength fueled the urgency building inside Brooks. There was no way he was in charge.

Brooks ripped his mouth from Rogan's and stared at him in astonishment. Even with the sexiest female companion, Brooks hadn't experienced this consuming desire. "I've never...."

"I have you, Mate. Nothing is off-limits for fate. We can take this slow," Rogan said, squaring his shoulders.

"Fuck that." Brooks grabbed Rogan's shirt and attempted to haul him forward. It was like trying to move a boulder. He only succeeded in pulling himself toward the shifter.

Rogan didn't allow him to think. He wrapped his arms around Brooks and pressed his mouth to his neck. When he bit the vulnerable spot at the curve of Brooks's shoulder, Brooks shivered as desire flared hotter inside him at that sensation. He rolled his head to the side to give him more access. Rogan's hands slipped under his fitted T-shirt to caress his abs before pushing the fabric higher.

"This has to come off, Mate. I need to look at you," Rogan growled and retreated a step to rip Brooks's shirt off.

Brooks stilled as Rogan checked him out, trying not to flex too obviously. Thoughts flew through his mind. Brooks wasn't a gym rat but preferred to exercise by hard work. His body was strong. Women seemed to find him handsome, but who knew what attracted a man?

"Damn! Unwrapping presents is now my favorite activity." The desire that shone from the shifter's eyes reassured him that he wasn't disappointed. Rogan didn't wait for him to ask. He reached over his back and grabbed a handful of his own shirt to drag it over his head.

"Fuck. What do you have? One percent body fat?" Why did he want to trace those grooves in Rogan's torso with his tongue?

"Dragon," Rogan reminded him. "Let me seal the entrance before you distract me completely."

Rogan walked toward a large metal disk that had to weigh a ton. The muscles in his back flexed as he rolled it to cover the flaming entrance. With that done, Rogan stalked toward Brooks, making him feel like prey. He loved it until Rogan leaned over to throw him over his shoulder. The shifter carried him easily away from the entrance.

"Rogan. I get it. You're strong. I can walk." Confusion filled Brooks's mind. Why was he enjoying this?

"The beast inside me needs this, Brooks. Besides, it's a faster way to get you to my bed." Rogan reached up to whack Brooks's ass.

Even through his heavy denim pants, Brooks felt that sting. He definitely didn't expect the twitch of his semi-erect cock. "Hey!"

"Spanking your bottom will happen, Mate."

"I don't think so. Who gets turned on by that?" Brooks tried to bluff.

Rogan laughed. "I can smell your desire, Mate. You have no secrets from me. The connection between most mates is strong. Ours is legendary."

Brooks had a quick upside-down tour of the dragon's

refuge. It was not what he'd expected inside a mountain. There were no cobwebs or creatures. He wanted to see more, but the sensation of the shifter's muscles moving under his weight mesmerized him. He shook his head, attempting to clear his mind. It didn't help.

He steadied himself by gripping Rogan's hips. The man's butt was epic. Brooks had always considered himself a breast man. Maybe that hadn't changed. Rogan must have enjoyed female mates. Maybe that was a connection between them.

Rogan walked through a doorway and stopped. A fraction of a second later, he leaned forward and dropped Brooks onto a soft surface. He bounced once and sat up.

"A warning would be nice. You don't want me to have a heart attack," Brooks groused.

Rogan stripped Brooks's shoes off and tossed them away. His socks followed quickly. Rogan crawled over him on the bed and sat on his thighs to unfasten his jeans.

"Whoa!" Brooks protested and backed up. His cock went into full alert as Rogan's fingers carefully pulled his zipper open.

"Stop?" Rogan asked, searching Brooks's face.

Brooks slowly shook his head. He curled up off the bed to kiss the magnetic figure looming over him. As their lips met, Rogan slid his hand into Brooks's jeans. Brooks gasped into his mouth when the shifter's fingers wrapped around his cock and squeezed.

"You need to be naked now," Rogan growled and released him to slide off the bottom of the bed. Rogan wrapped his hands around his mate's ankles and pulled Brooks to the edge of the bed before helping him stand. Quickly, he stripped Brooks's jeans and briefs from his body.

"Mate," Rogan complimented in a low voice, heavy with desire.

Rogan

"I want to see you too," Brooks said and stepped forward to unfasten Rogan's jeans. The shifter brushed his hands away, taking over. In seconds, he stood nude as Brooks admired his chiseled form. The power in Rogan's body was unmistakable.

"Women must go crazy over you," Brooks said and shook his head at the ridiculous statement. He was floundering and couldn't even come up with something intelligent to say.

"Brooks. I do not notice how anyone reacts to me. The only person I'm interested in is my mate. You."

Brooks could hear the truth echoing in that statement. He nodded, telling himself inside he could trust Rogan. All that escaped from his mind as Rogan moved.

Holding his gaze, Rogan dropped to his knees in front of Brooks. He stroked his large hands up Brooks's thighs. Rogan leaned forward to exhale a warm breath a fraction of an inch from Brooks's erection before running the tip of his tongue from the base to the broad head.

Brooks couldn't believe the overwhelming pleasure that threatened his control. His cock jerked in reaction to the caress. Off-balance from that lick, Brooks wrapped his hands around Rogan's broad shoulders, holding on to steady himself as he widened his stance. Upping the sensations, Rogan cupped Brooks's buttocks, pulling him forward as he opened his mouth to draw Brooks's shaft inside.

Struggling to not thrust his hips toward his mate, Brooks reveled in the erotic scene happening in front of him. The view struck a deep desire he hadn't known he enjoyed. This felt better than right. It felt essential.

Rogan's tongue swirled along the underside of Brooks's shaft, pushing his control as if it were his first time. Clamping down on his arousal, Brooks tried to think of anything else. He couldn't come like a virgin within minutes of being caressed.

Relax, Mate. Enjoy. I'm nowhere near finished with you.

Rogan underlined that statement by tugging gently on Brooks's sac as he sucked hard.

"Ahhh!"

Rogan's touch pushed his arousal further into dangerous territory. His knees shook as he struggled to regain his balance. Rogan's hands on his butt supported his weight easily.

Too soon, Rogan's hot mouth released him, and he pressed a kiss to his still hard shaft. Rogan dragged his soft beard to Brooks's thigh. There, he nipped the tender skin.

Brooks met his gaze in surprise.

I'm very glad to have found you, mate. Rogan rose to embrace Brooks, pressing their shafts together. *Are you ready for me to make love to you fully? If you need time....*

"I don't know what's going on here, but I can feel inside me that this is right. Be gentle?"

You are my mate, Brooks. I will take good care of you.

"What do I do?"

Onto the bed, My Adventurer. Let's go explore. Rogan stepped back to guide Brooks to stretch out in the center of the giant bed. Following closely behind him, Rogan joined him. Brooks turned to him, eager to explore his mate.

The urgency between them rebuilt as they kissed and explored their mate's body. Each searched for those special spots that brought the other pleasure. Brooks gained confidence as Rogan responded to his touch with soft moans and mental praise.

Mate, you are driving me crazy. I want you now.

"Yes. Please." Brooks allowed Rogan to shift him onto his hands and knees. He closed his eyes in ecstasy as Rogan applied lubricant to his tight opening before dipping inside. The sensation of his fingers moving in and out of him threatened to make him spill.

When Rogan's thick cock pressed inside, Brooks grabbed handfuls of the comforter below him, crumpling it in his fists. Rogan slowly stretched his tight passage without hesitation. With the enormous shifter wrapped around him, Brooks could only submit. The burn of his entrance increased the desire already filling Brooks. He'd had female partners stimulate him here with their fingers, but this felt totally different. Rogan dominated him.

When their bodies met fully, Rogan kissed and then bit Brooks's shoulder. *You are incredible.*

"I need you to move," Brooks demanded, making Rogan chuckle.

Your wish is my command.

The flurry of thrusts that followed erased anything Brooks had ever learned about sex. The mate bond made this so much more than simple desire and attraction. The link grew and deepened until it shimmered around them. A massive climax shook Brooks as he and the shifter melded together, creating something completely new.

"Rogan!" He panicked at the intimate sensation.

The mating bond has snapped fully into place, My Adventurer. Enjoy. It will only get better.

"This is going to kill me," Brooks muttered as he collapsed onto the bed.

Not for a couple hundred years or more, hopefully.

Brooks couldn't process that statement. They lay together until their heart rates settled closer to normal. He grabbed Rogan's arm when the shifter eased away.

"I'll never leave you, Adventurer. I need to care for you. Come to the bathroom."

Brooks appreciated that the darkness concealed his flaming cheeks as the shifter tended to him. Stumbling with weariness, he allowed Rogan to guide him back to bed and tuck him under the covers. As soon as his mate pulled him close, Brooks tumbled into sleep with his head on Rogan's hard shoulder. His lips curved as he registered Rogan's soft message.

Welcome home, Mate.

Chapter 3

Rogan kissed his mate's sweet lips as Brooks roused. He wanted to learn everything about his mate. First, he needed to take care of him. When those brown eyes opened to lock with his, Rogan sent him waves of positivity. He kissed Brooks until he responded with eagerness before lifting his mouth away.

"Good morning, mate."

"Um... Hi. I should go to the bathroom," Brooks said self-consciously, as he eased away from Rogan and slipped from under the covers.

"Wait, Brooks."

His mate didn't listen but fled toward the open doorway. Rogan followed quickly and caught up with Brooks when his new mate jolted to a stop, panting in pain as the mate bond required that they stay close. He hugged Brooks and held him close as he recovered. Rogan hated to see his mate suffering.

"The mate bond is complete, but it wants us together. We'll need to stay close until it relaxes, My Adventurer."

"I can't even go to piss alone?"

Rogan allowed himself to smile since Brooks couldn't see

him. "Of course. This darn bedroom is too large. Let's go into the bathroom. I'll run a bath while you use the toilet."

His mate's grumbles enchanted him. Brooks was not a morning person. Rogan wrapped an arm around him and guided the sleepy man into the bathroom. While he used the separate toilet area, Rogan triggered the ancient water heater and started the water in the enormous tub.

When Brooks emerged, Rogan handed him a new toothbrush already spread with paste. "Want this? We'll go get your things soon."

"I don't have much. Only what I can carry easily. I don't hang around anyplace too long."

Rogan recognized that as a warning. His mate didn't realize his life had drastically changed when they'd met. Now, his adventuring would happen in tandem. Without replying, Rogan stroked a reassuring hand down Brooks's back before using the toilet himself.

Exiting the small room, he found Brooks leaning on the wall next to the door. He was afraid to roam too far. Rogan took his hand and led him to the bath. As he passed the sink, he smiled at the sight of two toothbrushes together. Quietly, he celebrated finding his mate, allowing the positive vibes to seep into their connection. Brooks's tense shoulders lowered a bit.

"Step in, Brooks. We'll soak for a bit," Rogan suggested, holding his arm to help him step in.

"I'm not an infant," Brooks said and yanked away.

"That's enough. Unless you want to sit in the bath with a punished bottom, you'll get that attitude under control."

The flare of arousal in Brooks's eyes told Rogan a lot. Brooks squashed that desire quickly, but it was too late. "I suspect you're probably sore. The warm water will help."

Without another word, Brooks settled into the tub. When Rogan followed him, Brooks scooted over to the side.

"You're joining me?" He obviously wasn't used to sharing a tub with anyone.

"Yes. We will share most things." Rogan pulled him close and wrapped an arm around him before leaning against the porcelain. When Brooks relaxed next to him, Rogan rubbed his shoulder reassuringly but stayed quiet, allowing his mate to think.

"You'd spank me? I didn't consider that I'd face abuse."

"No abuse, Brooks. Punishment if you earn it."

Brooks turned to search his face for a clue to Rogan's mood and intention. "I'm not a kid, Rogan. I mean, you're old, but I'm an adult."

Rogan controlled his expression. Brooks was pushing for control when he didn't want it. Was this why he'd roamed for so many years? "You're fully grown, Brooks. I appreciate every inch of you. I also suspect that despite your grown-up status, there's a Little inside you who would love the freedom to live as well."

"Little? What are you're talking about?"

Rogan wouldn't let him hide. "You do realize that our bond makes all things easier. Sex. Our relationship. My ability to see the real you. And yours to see me."

He could almost hear the wheels in Brooks's bright brain churning from those details. His mate sat quietly next to him as they basked in the warm water. Finally, Brooks whispered, "Can you read my mind?"

"Only if you allow me. I can, however, pick up a lot from your actions and the emotions I sense wafting off you. I also suspect most of the mates have been Little. You might be an exception, but I don't think so."

"Skye is Little. I mean, I noticed she sits on her mates' laps. I figured Oldrik and Ardon were just taking care of her. Don't get any ideas. I'm not sitting on your lap," Brooks declared.

"You will if you need that closeness. And I suspect you'll enjoy it. If that makes you uncomfortable in public, we'll adjust until we find what works for you. At home, you will be whoever you're meant to be."

Rogan knew Brooks needed to digest that information. He sat up, drawing Brooks with him. "Come here. Let me wash your back. It gives me a good excuse to get my hands on you."

"Do you need an excuse?" Brooks challenged.

"No. But I want you to enjoy our time together," Rogan told him quietly. He wouldn't allow Brooks to hide from him. "Were you unhappy last night?"

After a long second's pause, Brooks shook his head. "No. It was magical. I've never experienced anything like that."

Rogan smiled at him and pulled his face close to reward him with a passionate kiss. "Thank you for telling me the truth."

He helped Brooks shift slightly to sit in front of him. Dispensing some of his favorite bodywash, Rogan spread it over his mate's back. The feel of Brooks's toned muscles under his fingertips rekindled the arousal that had simmered just under the surface since Rogan had met his mate. Brooks's soft moan of enjoyment fueled that excitement. He took his time before splashing water over his mate's back to rinse away the suds.

Rogan pressed a kiss to Brooks's shoulder before whispering. "Turn around, Adventurer."

He helped him change position and washed his chest. To Rogan's delight, Brooks sat still, giving him free access. Rogan splashed water to rinse the soap away. When he shifted to Brooks's thighs, his mate jerked and slid on the porcelain surface.

"Whoa, Mate," Rogan said, quickly wrapping his hands around Brooks's waist to steady him. His fingertips brushed across his mate's erection. Rogan's caresses had also affected him.

Brooks's quick inhale made Rogan abandon his mate's thighs to concentrate on another area. He wrapped his fingers around Brooks's cock and pulled from root to tip, drawing a deep groan from Brooks. He repeated the motion, only stopping when Brooks slid again as he tried to thrust into Rogan's grip.

Stabilizing him, Rogan whispered, "Let's get you cleaned up, and we'll climb out of this tub before you're hurt."

"How come you don't slip?" Brooks asked.

"Scales."

Rogan let him think about that without explaining as he washed his mate's legs and feet. "Up on your knees, mate."

Brooks followed his instruction and asked a second later. "Scales? What do you mean?"

"Dragons have scales," Rogan reminded him as he smoothed soap between Brooks's buttocks.

"I can do that," Brooks protested and grabbed for the tub's edge when he lost his balance.

"Already finished," Rogan informed him. "Sit back down to rinse."

While having something to do distracted his mate, Rogan washed Brooks's balls and thick cock. He explored his mate's shaft, searching for the most responsive spots. Feeling Brooks's pulse through the thick veins along the underside, Rogan celebrated his mate's life and vitality. He met Brooks's gaze when his mate stroked a hand through his hair.

"This is real?"

"Yes, Adventurer. This is your new journey. You've searched for something and run away for too long. Is this what you need?" Rogan asked, caressing him. The slick soap provided a lubricant for his hand. He quickened his pace and wrapped his arm around Brooks to hold him in place against him.

"Oh, fuck!" Brooks protested. "Searched? Run? I can't think when you're touching me."

"That's the way it should be. Consider about your motivation later, Brooks. For now, feel."

"I could...."

"You can pleasure me next time, mate. Enjoy now," Rogan instructed, tightening his grip around Brooks's waist and cock.

"Fuck!" Brooks shouted. His voice echoed on the hard tiled surfaces around them as he spilled into the water.

Rogan coaxed the last of the sensations from him before releasing him. Brooks turned, seeking his reassurance, and Rogan pulled him close. Wrapped around his mind-blown mate, Rogan closed his eyes as he pressed his forehead to Brooks's temple. He thanked the fates for bringing him such a treasure.

When Brooks shifted against him, Rogan said, "I'll get out and help you." He'd just stepped out when Brooks chose to move immediately. Rogan quickly scooped him out of the tub and set him safely on the rug.

"Hey!" Brooks protested, rubbing his butt when Rogan sharply slapped his bottom.

"That's a warning. Follow directions, Adventurer."

"I won't be a puppet, Rogan. That's not who I am."

Rogan schooled his face to keep his amusement from showing as he grabbed a fluffy towel to rub over his mate's skin. "I know you are independent, Brooks. I do not wish to erase that from your personality. I wouldn't change anything about you. You will, however, heed my instructions to keep from endangering yourself. If you don't, a spanking will help you learn."

Heat flared in Brooks's gaze. "That's not going to happen."

"It will, and you will simultaneously hate and love your spankings. Now, we are both hungry. Let's dress, and we'll head to breakfast."

"I'd like to go get my things," Brooks said.

"After breakfast, we'll take care of that."

"Can we use the front door this time instead of the ring of deadly flames?" Brooks requested.

"Of course, Mate. We'll save the waterfall entrance for emergencies. How about I give you a quick tour of your new home so you'll be able to find your way around."

"Thanks. This place is huge."

When they were dressed, Rogan showed him the main areas of the mansion, highlighting rooms that they would use frequently as well as the entrances and main corridors. He hated that Keres had negatively impacted Brooks's arrival. Hopefully, making new happy memories would eliminate any scary flashbacks. Rogan stressed that nothing had ever penetrated his deceptively beautiful fortress and Brooks would be safe here.

While Keres no longer lurked in the area, Rogan had alerted the other members of the horde of the attack. When he could leave his mate to meet with the others alone, all the dragons minus Keres would gather to discuss their options for dealing with the black dragon's growing menace to the horde. Rogan regretted this day had come. Keres had been a member of the horde for centuries. Unfortunately, something needed to happen. Soon.

Chapter 4

Despite his vow to never ride a dragon again, Brooks clung to the red dragon's neck as he flew toward the old city center of Wyvern. He focused on the beauty of the view. Everything looked so small below him.

Brooks hugged Rogan a bit harder at the thought of tumbling from this distance. Thank goodness heights had never scared him. Not that Rogan would let him get hurt. Rogan had taken to extraordinary measures to keep him safe when Keres had attacked. His hand smoothed over the glistening scales that protected the dragon's hide. Rogan was beautiful.

An image of Rogan's chiseled body popped into his brain. Pure power. It boggled his mind how attracted he was to the dragon shifter. Brooks would never have even fantasized about any of the events that had occurred. First mated, then a relationship with another man, and finally finding himself dominated by a force he craved more than Brooks wanted to admit.

Are you okay, Adventurer?

Rogan's deep voice inside his mind made Brooks shiver. Even his message was sexy. *I'm fine*, he answered, still testing their connection. *All the stuff that's happened is tumbling around in my skull.*

Change is hard. I hope you'll decide this is a positive branch in your path.

Brooks didn't answer that. The ties that connected them grew stronger with each moment that passed. His feelings also deepened. His mind just needed to catch up.

A wave of reassurance floated over his thoughts, making him smile. Brooks savored Rogan's mental caress. Interacting with him showed Brooks the emptiness in his life. Perhaps that unfulfilled part of him had caused his roaming.

Had he always been bisexual? Could he have not known himself to that extent?

You thought that strongly, Mate. Perhaps you're worrying about something that's easily answered. Perhaps our sexual parts aren't the important component here. The connection supersedes everything. You could be purple and me from the moon. Our mating bond would still tie us together.

That idea struck Brooks between the eyes. Nothing was important except for their fated union. His self-questioning faded away.

Thank you, Rogan.

I've been around a few more years than you, Brooks. That has given me a lot of time to consider the mate bond from different perspectives. The most important thing for you to remember is that I treasure you.

A comfortable silence fell between them until Brooks spotted his grandmother's home in the oldest section of Wyvern. Still perfectly preserved, the house had belonged to the family since the beginning of the town. *There, Rogan. Ahead of us. That's weird. The door is painted red now. Where should we stop so you can shift?*

Thanks to no traffic, I'll settle on the street in front of the door.

Rogan trumpeted a warning before landing smoothly in front of the red portal. Elenore opened the door and stood with her hands at her heart as Brooks slid off to land on the cobblestones. A round of enthusiastic applause sounded, surprising him. Six neighbors had noted the large creature arriving and had gathered to celebrate.

Not sure what to do in the spotlight, Brooks froze in place until Rogan's powerful arm wrapped around his waist. He definitely wasn't used to being the center of attention.

"Thank you, everyone," Elenore called to those celebrating with them.

"Yes, thank you," Brooks echoed, wanting only to escape into the house.

"Come, Mate. Let's go talk to your grandmother," Rogan suggested and guided him to the entrance.

"Red dragon, as the Guardian of the Battlefield family, I welcome you into our home. Please enter," Elenore said politely.

"Thank you, Elenore of Battlefield. I am pleased to be mated to your family," Rogan told her as they stepped inside. "Thank you for declaring our union at your portal."

"Of course." Elenore rushed forward to hug her grandson. "Brooks, are you okay?"

"I'm confused but happy. Rogan is helping me adjust. Becoming a dragon's mate was not on my radar."

"Of course not. It is very rare. May I make you some lunch?"

Brooks glanced at Rogan, hoping his mate would pick up that he wanted to get out of there as quickly as possible. Suddenly, he simply wanted to be alone with his mate.

"No thank you, Elenore. I would prefer to guard my mate at home," Rogan answered.

"Of course. Brooks will show you his room where his things are," Elenore said with a smile.

Heading toward the hallway, Brooks took Rogan's hand. "It's this way."

When they were alone, Brooks told him, "I'll get my stuff together. I don't have a lot."

Walking to the closet, Brooks grabbed a couple of pairs of jeans hanging inside. He threw those on the bed as Rogan stepped closer to the bookshelves. Keeping an eye on his mate, Brooks found a satchel and filled it with underwear and T-shirts. He grabbed his one button-down shirt and added that to the contents before stashing jeans inside as well. Taking advantage of his mate's distraction, Brooks grabbed a soft item from under his pillow and tucked that under his clothes before zipping the bag closed.

"You have many mementos from your travels," Rogan observed.

"Yeah. I never bring home anything big or valuable. Only special things that remind me of places I've been."

"I bet this red rock came from Arizona," Rogan guessed, holding up a small pebble.

"Yes. I liked its shape. It feels good in your hand."

Rogan closed his fingers around the stone and smiled. "It does."

He replaced it on the shelf and picked up a black velvet box. "And this?"

"The ring I never gave to my long-time girlfriend. She made an ultimatum, and I went to buy her an engagement ring."

"You couldn't give it to her?"

Sensing something in Rogan's voice, Brooks studied his

mate's face as he talked. "Something stopped me. I couldn't understand it then. Maybe this was why?" Brooks guessed. "It was a while ago. She's not in town anymore." Did he see relief on Rogan's face?

"Something inside you, definitely. Individuals who choose another path before meeting their fated mate can have happy lives. I will admit, I'm glad I won't run into a woman who tried to manipulate you into getting married."

Brooks nodded. "I kept it to remind myself that I need to do what my heart tells me is correct. Maybe I should take that with me," he suggested, holding out his hand for it.

Rogan put it on his palm. "Remembering to pay attention to the voice here," he said, pressing his hand to Brooks's heart, "instead of heeding what the outside world says you should is wise."

His fingers curled to capture a handful of Brooks's shirt. Rogan tugged him close and lowered his head to kiss him hard. When he lifted his head, Brooks clung to him. "Thank you for listening to your heart, Adventurer."

"I made the right choice," Brooks said, feeling that conviction inside. He smiled at Rogan before pressing his lips back to his mate's.

That kiss became more as the heat swelled between them. Rogan ripped his mouth away finally and set Brooks a short distance from him.

"If you don't want me to take you on that bed, you'll stay over there," Rogan warned.

The growl of his low voice made Brooks smile. Who knew that a dragon's self-control could be challenged? He enjoyed having the power to affect Rogan.

"Let's go talk to your grandmother. She needs to hear that you're okay," Rogan told him.

"Good idea. She'll worry. She raised me when my parents

passed away young." Brooks grabbed his sneakers and his journal. After stuffing them into his satchel, he fastened the buckles and slung the leather bag over his shoulders.

They found Elenore in the kitchen in front of a large tome. It started glowing as soon as Brooks entered the room.

"It recognizes you. I've updated our family information to reflect our honor in contributing a mate," she said, waving a hand at the enormous book.

She stood and walked toward Brooks, studying his face. Brooks hoped his lips weren't as swollen as they felt after Rogan's kisses. "Are you happy?"

"Yes, Grandma. It's a lot to get adjusted to, but Rogan is helping me. This feels right," Brooks assured her.

Elenore cupped his jaw. "Let me get you something." She disappeared before Brooks could stop her. He shrugged as he met Rogan's gaze.

When she returned, she handed Brooks a small jar. "Put this on your abrasions. Your skin isn't used to Rogan's beard."

Can the floor open up and swallow me? His cheeks heated, and Brooks looked helplessly at Rogan. His mate stepped forward to tuck the cream into the satchel slung over Brooks's shoulder.

"Thank you, Elenore. I will bring him back to visit you," Rogan promised.

"I would enjoy that." Elenore rushed forward to hug her grandson. "Be happy."

Brooks nodded and walked to the front door. Once outside, he stood on the curb as Rogan shifted into his dragon form. He noticed the neighbors peeking out their windows and stepping outside. He couldn't fault them. Rogan was magical.

Climbing up on his back, Brooks celebrated he was getting better at mounting the dragon. Just then, his boots slipped on a scale, making him slide. Brooks grabbed for a better handhold.

A powerful wing pressed against his side, balancing Brooks in place and allowing him to recover. Brooks rolled his eyes at himself, feeling embarrassed in front of the audience that watched.

Careful, Mate.

Quickly, he scrambled into place and wrapped his arms around Rogan's neck. The red dragon launched himself into the air without delay and soared into the sky. The faint sound of applause reached Brooks's ears. He was proud of his community for cheering for the dragons.

Wyverns had returned to their celebration of the dragons who guarded their city. Brooks had experienced life outside the protected city after the end of technology. He'd also heard the stories of new arrivals. As supplies grew scarce, the worst of people appeared.

Think happy thoughts, mate. Want to enter through the fire ring or the front lawn?

The memory of that scary plunge through the waterfall and into a fiery ring ricocheted into his mind. Brooks shook his head to rid himself of that visual.

Front lawn, it is.

Chapter 5

With each moment he spent with Rogan, Brooks felt more at ease. It was almost as if threads of connection stitched between the dragon shifter and Brooks over time. Since they were unable to be far away from each other, Rogan was a genius in coming up with activities for them to do together.

Today, they walked around his mountain exploring. It helped burn off pent-up energy and tension. Brooks loved Rogan, but being with anyone this much was a challenge. He'd always been solitary.

"How long does the mate bond last?" Brooks asked as he thought about it.

"Our bond will exist until one of us passes. Why?" Rogan looked at him in concern.

"Just wondering. It's new to me, of course. I figured I should learn more."

"You can ask me any question you have, Brooks. Are you uncomfortable here with me?"

Hearing the concern in his mate's voice, Brooks rushed to explain. "No. Not really. I mean... It's a big change for me. I'm used to being out in the world—going different places."

"Have you always enjoyed traveling?" Rogan asked, as he extended a hand to help Brooks climb over a fence into the livestock field.

"I liked being at home as a kid with my parents. I guess that's normal. But when I got out of school, I explored outside of Wyvern."

"Didn't your parents worry about you?"

"Oh, they were gone by then."

"Gone?" Rogan echoed.

"Yes. I'm sorry. I thought I'd told you. My folks were killed in a car accident when I was fifteen."

"That's awful. I didn't realize that happened when you were so young. You went to live with your grandmother after they died?"

"Yes. She was awesome. I'm sure having a teenager eat her out of house and home wasn't what she would have chosen." Brooks laughed. It sounded hollow even to his ears. He'd always worried about being a burden to his grandmother.

"I'm sure losing your parents was quite a blow. I don't know Elenore well, but she's a very strong woman who seems to value family."

"Yes. It was tough on her. I tried to make it easier for both of us. You know, find lots to keep myself busy, so I wasn't moping around, cluttering her space."

"I noticed you look a lot like your father."

"Grandma calls us twins. She often said I reminded her of him as a kid. I caught her staring at me sometimes with a sad expression. She would shake it off when she saw me notice. It was easier on her if I was out of the house. I missed my folks a lot, too."

Brooks noticed the sheep shied from them—Rogan especially—as they walked through the field. They weren't dumb. Animals could sense a predator close to them.

"Maybe having you in her life made the pain more bearable. She hadn't really lost all of her son with you around," Rogan suggested.

"Maybe." Brooks hadn't thought of it like that.

"So, starting after the death of your folks, you stayed away from home?"

"Don't make it sound like something psychological. I always enjoyed exploring new areas. My folks loved visiting different places and finding spots off the beaten path," Brooks said defensively.

"Of course, it's nothing weird. We all have things we like and dislike. It sounds like being an adventurer is hardwired into your DNA."

"Yeah. That's true. Look." Brooks pointed to a small opening in the mountainside. "Is that a cave? Have you ever been inside?"

"You've got a good eye. It's a passage that leads to an underground pool. Icy cold water straight from the mountaintop."

"Can we go check it out? Escape from the sun for a while?"

"Of course. It's dark in there, but I can give us some light if you don't mind my eyes glowing red."

"That's handy. I don't need a flashlight when I'm with you," Brooks said.

"Come on then. Let's go spelunking. Stay close. I'll guide you through."

Brooks loved how easily they worked together. Of course, Rogan's brute strength meant every physical challenge was much easier, but somehow his mate anticipated any problem he might have. "Have you been in here with others?" He didn't ask about another mate specifically, but that was what Brooks wondered.

"Good lord, no. Most of my female mates weren't into

spiders or other creepy crawlers that might exist in a cave," Rogan told him with a chuckle.

Squashing the jealousy that burst inside him at the thought of others sharing Rogan's life, Brooks forced himself to focus on the present. The past shouldn't matter, right?

Bugs. Rogan had mentioned stuff living in the passage. Peering through the darkness, Brooks hoped he was kidding. "There are insects in here?"

"Not too many since the bats moved in."

"Bats?" Brooks hunkered down from the high ceiling.

"Don't worry. They sense I'm like a bat on steroids. They're definitely not venturing close to us."

"That makes sense." Still, Brooks was going to look up for a while.

As they got away from the opening, it grew darker. A dim, red light filled the inside of the cavern. Brooks looked at Rogan in wonder and saw his eyes glowing like something out of a horror movie. "Okay. That's a bit frightening."

"Do we need to go back?" Rogan asked immediately.

"No. It's okay. You warned me."

"We're almost there, Adventurer. I'd hate for you to miss this now. Try looking toward your feet instead of at me," Rogan suggested.

"You said the ladies were afraid of the spiders. Your first mate, the guy, he didn't come in here?"

"Ian? No, he never visited this spot. The pool has existed for hundreds of years, but the entrance only appeared about two hundred years ago. It wasn't here for him to forge through. Although he would have taken an axe or a sledgehammer to the cliff face if he'd known it was there."

"You miss him." Brooks glanced up at Rogan and slid when his foot hit a slick spot.

"Careful, Mate." The dragon shifter lifted him easily and

set him on a safer patch of ground before answering. "I remember all my mates fondly. Ian was a character. When he passed, he was ready. Even if I'd been able to extend his life longer, I wouldn't have."

"Because he was suffering?" Brooks asked as a shiver ran down his spine. Living longer sounded great, but he definitely didn't want to stick around when he was falling apart.

"No. He was healthy until the end. He was just prepared to leave this world. His siblings' grandchildren had lived and passed. People didn't survive until their eighties or older back then. He didn't want to see another generation buried. Ian was 154 on his last birthday. To witness so many leave this world wore on him."

"I can understand that."

"One more corner to turn. Get ready."

The air gushed out of Brooks's lungs at the sight of the gorgeous pool. Small bits of light glowed from the cave walls, giving the area an ethereal glow. "Wow, this is amazing."

"It really is. We can take a dip in the water. It's refreshing and crystal clear." Rogan whipped his shirt over his head and tossed it to a flat stone next to the pool.

"I can see that." Brooks allowed himself to be drawn toward Rogan, who pulled his mate's shirt off as well and added it to the pile. He bucked backward when Rogan unfastened the button at the top of his jeans.

"You can't swim?" Rogan asked.

"Like a fish," Brooks corrected him. "Sorry. It's weird to have someone undress me."

"You'll need to get used to that, unless there's some trauma in your past I should know about?" Rogan probed.

"No. Nothing like that," Brooks rushed to assure him.

"I'm glad." Rogan tugged him into his arms to give him a hug and a light kiss. "It's okay, Brooks, to let yourself be cared for. You've been out there in the world, doing everything yourself. What would happen if I help?"

Brooks shook his head and shrugged. "Nothing bad. I trust you."

"I'm glad to hear that. I'll tell you what. How about if you undress me this time?"

He hadn't expected that. Brooks liked that idea. "Can I touch you?"

"The dragon will only allow me to be submissive to a certain point. Then, he will take over," Rogan warned before adding. "We'd both love to feel your touch." He glided a few inches back from Brooks.

Grinning at the opportunity, Brooks ran his fingers along Rogan's waistband, loving the contraction of Rogan's chiseled abs under his caress. Rogan was sheer male beauty and strength. He popped open the button, and Rogan's heavy shaft twitched against his fly. He loved that his mate responded to him eagerly. Brooks carefully pulled the zipper down, releasing his growing erection. Wrapping his fingers around Rogan's thickness, he guided his cock outside the confining fabric.

"Are you taking off my clothes or getting acquainted?" Rogan asked in a gruff tone that teased as it revealed his arousal.

"Both?" Brooks asked.

"Clothes first, Mate."

"Okay." He drew out that answer, hoping Rogan would get the hint. He might want more after that.

"Clothes, Brooks."

Brooks nodded and pushed Rogan's jeans over his hips. His mate never wore anything under the form-fitting, heavy denim. He had to admit Rogan looked especially good coming and leaving. Brooks rolled his eyes at that last thought. Rogan looked much better than good when he came.

He leaned over to slide the material down to Rogan's ankles and found himself close to Rogan's erection. Unable to control his urge, Brooks licked it. He loved the salty taste of his mate's skin.

"Pants, Brooks," Rogan reminded him.

Quickly, he squatted to the ground and helped Rogan step out of his jeans and shoes. Brooks rubbed his cheek against Rogan's shaft repeatedly, as if it were an accident.

Rogan slid his powerful hands under Brooks' arms and hauled him to his feet.

"Eep!" A squeak escaped from his lips.

"You dare too much, Mate." Rogan growled as he lifted him and tossed Brooks into the pond.

Brooks sputtered to the surface, brushing his hair out of his eyes. His teeth chattered from the icy water. "This isn't refreshing. It's like swimming in the North Pole!"

"When a dragon goes in first, he can warm it with his body temperature."

Rogan waded inside and swam to Brooks's side. Encircling his mate in his arms, Rogan shared his heat. "Better?"

"Yes. Thank you. I'm glad I still have my pants and shoes on. I might have lost a toe to frostbite," Brooks exaggerated wildly.

Rogan laughed. "Teasing dragons has consequences."

"I'll never do it again," Brooks promised.

"Yes, you will, and I'll enjoy it." Rogan wrapped his hand around the back of Brooks's head and drew him in for a kiss. That exchange warmed every part of Brooks. When he lifted his head, Rogan's eyes twinkled. "Want me to throw you one more time?"

"Yes. Then chase me. I think I'll like that part."

"Your pants come off when I catch you," Rogan warned.

"You have to grab me first," Brooks challenged. "I'm a fish in the water."

"Indeed? Let's test your theory about how survival of the fittest works. Hold your breath."

Rogan gathered him to his chest and tossed Brooks high into the air toward the other side of the pool. Immediately, the dragon shifter cut a path through the water without an ounce of effort. Rogan stood a foot away from Brooks's landing spot when he splashed down.

Before Brooks could stop his descent and swim for the surface, Rogan's powerful arms scooped him back up to throw him over his shoulder. As Brooks refilled his lungs, Rogan stripped off his shoes, jeans, and boxer briefs. They landed with wet splooshes on the stones where they had stood earlier.

"How did you get over here so fast?" Brooks asked, panting, as he tried to push himself away from Rogan's shoulder.

"Flying through water is close to air, Mate." Rogan stretched his wings out behind him, fluttering them slightly before returning them into wherever all his dragon parts disappeared when he was in human form. He smacked Brooks on his now bare bottom. "Never make a bet with a dragon. It won't turn out well for you."

"Ouch! And I'll remember not to challenge you to a race."

"Smart." Rogan delivered another stinging slap to his butt before tossing him through the air.

Brooks surfaced, sputtering and laughing at the same time. He launched a vicious splash attack at the dragon shifter, pushing so much water he couldn't see past it himself. When Rogan didn't respond, he paused to check out the effect. His mate had disappeared.

A hand wrapped around his ankle and gave a warning tug. Brooks inhaled quickly before Rogan pulled him under the water. The dragon shifter wrapped his arms around Brooks and pushed off the bottom, launching them explosively out of the water and splashing back down into it.

The antics continued until Brooks was exhausted. Rogan didn't even breathe heavily, to Brooks's dismay. "Don't you ever get tired?"

"Rarely." He winked at Brooks. "Endurance is one of a dragon's best qualities."

Brooks cursed his reaction as his cheeks heated with embarrassment as his mind flashed back to their intimate interactions. He definitely couldn't deny that Rogan's thorough lovemaking certainly exceeded Brooks's expectations. "You're bad," he whispered.

"And you're adorable," Rogan whispered. "I am a very lucky dragon. Want to go home and rest?"

"Why do I think rest is the last thing on your mind?" Brooks muttered.

"Probably because your thoughts are as equally as erotic as mine." This time, when Rogan's hand struck Brooks's bottom, it returned to squeeze his cheek suggestively. "Then a nap for you. We need to keep your strength up."

Brooks nodded eagerly.

Chapter 6

A few days later, Rogan considered his mate as they sat on the patio overlooking Wyvern. He could tell Brooks was getting antsy. He would have to think of something new for his mate to do.

"How did you earn money as you traveled around?" Rogan asked casually.

"It didn't take much to survive. I did a bit of everything. My favorite job was in Wyvern. I was in charge of supplies in a warehouse. You know, tracking where all the supplies were and how many items were in that area."

A picture of his lair popped into Rogan's mind. He had the location of every single piece of his treasure memorized. Brooks didn't need to be privy to that information.

"Really? I might have a task for you. That is, if you're interested." Rogan dangled the opportunity in front of his mate.

"What is it? I don't like to sit around a lot." Brooks leaned forward eagerly

"Let me show you." Rogan stood and led Brooks into the mansion. He headed toward the more rustic part of the house built into his mountain. Stopping at a blank section of wall, he pressed several seemingly random spots. The rumble of grinding wheels reached them.

A passage slowly opened in front of them. Rogan extended out a hand to Brooks and led him inside the dark entrance. "Stand right there. I'll light a torch," he told his mate as the gears restarted, closing the room.

"I'm not moving," Brooks promised.

Igniting the first torch, Rogan then lit the closest to them. The pools of light revealed a section of the chamber. Brooks scanned the illuminated area.

"Is that a pile of gold?"

"Yes."

"Do you have any idea how much that is worth?" Brooks asked.

"I have a good idea."

"What's the job? Counting that pile?" Brooks joked.

"No. Weighing it would be much more efficient. I thought you might start with the weaponry."

"Weaponry? Like guns?"

"Think older," Rogan suggested.

"Spears?" Brooks guessed.

"Totally uncollectible. Wood disintegrates. Let me show you." Rogan led Brooks to a small outer chamber and lit the torch there.

When Brooks sneezed, Rogan regretted the dust in that section. Too much time had passed since he was in this room. Silvery hilts and ornately carved scabbards dimly reflected the light under the weight of the grime that had settled on the collection.

"No way. Those are swords. Is there a light saber room hidden in here somewhere?" Brooks demanded.

"They shatter too quickly," Rogan told him, shaking his head. "And they are worthless in a battle."

"You know how to fight?"

"Of course."

"Could you teach me?" Brooks asked.

"Yes. But only if you get these organized and counted for me."

"Should I take pictures for insurance?" Brooks asked.

"Dragon. No insurance needed."

"Oh, yeah. Anyone who tried to rob you is nuts."

Brooks scanned the items and asked, "Can you give me a brief lesson on types of swords so I can classify them? There are different types, right?"

Rogan showed him examples of claymores, sabers, rapiers, broadswords, and many more. Most were already grouped into categories, but a few had wandered into the wrong section. Rogan loved Brooks's quick mind. He was curious and loved learning.

"Hey! This one still has blood on it," Brooks called, holding up a katana.

Lifting it to his nose, Rogan sniffed at the last dusty remnants on the blade. "Mine. I remember this sword. The guy appeared, dressed all in black, like a ninja. He tried to climb up the mountain face but got stuck on a wicked outcropping of rock."

"Did you save him?"

"I flew by and flapped my wings to dislodge him."

"You knocked him down the cliff?"

"He was coming to steal my treasure," Rogan reminded him. "With that sword. I don't think he intended that weapon to be a tribute or trade. Especially when he got in a lucky shot as I flew by and struck a place where I'd lost a scale. I claimed his sword for that and dropped him a few hundred miles away."

"That seems fair," Brooks said with a nod and got started sorting and classifying the weaponry.

"Wait. Wear these," Rogan directed, handing Brooks a pair of metal-mesh gloves. "The edges are sharp." His mate rolled his eyes but followed directions.

They worked well together. Rogan took advantage of the close environment to kiss and caress Brooks often. After a couple of hours, they had many groupings stacked in piles. Rogan was impressed. Brooks had excellent ideas.

When Brooks sneezed five times in a row and had trouble catching his breath, Rogan knew they had been in the dusty chamber for too long. "Time to stop for the day."

"But we have more to do," Brooks pointed out.

"We have many days to organize this. For today, this is a good start." Rogan wrapped his arm around Brooks's waist and guided him out of the lair.

Once back in the hallway, Rogan looked down at his clothes. They were both completely filthy. "We need to get all this dust off. Think you can lead us to our room?"

"No problem," Brooks said confidently. "I've got the place memorized."

Impressively, Brooks only took a few wrong turns before reaching the bedroom. "This place is monstrous," he commented before sneezing a couple more times.

"We've got to get you cleaned up. Come on." Rogan shooed Brooks into the bathroom. He switched on the water as he addressed Brooks's previous statement. "The house is immense. You did a great job getting us around. I'm impressed."

Rogan tugged Brooks's shirt over his head. "I'll dump our clothes in the tub, so we don't spread this everywhere."

When he unbuttoned his mate's jeans, Rogan noticed Brooks pulled away slightly before relaxing and allowing

Rogan to undress him. "Thank you, Brooks. I enjoy taking care of you."

In a few minutes, he had revealed his mate's toned frame. "Jump in the shower and let the water rinse over you as I get these clothes off."

Brooks groaned in delight as the shower pelted down on him. "How do you have warm water?"

"There's an old-fashioned, fire-fueled water heater in the basement. It existed way before the electric and gas-powered ones came about."

"You held onto it all this time?" Brooks asked in disbelief.

"Dragons are notorious for hoarding things." Rogan grabbed a tube from the drawer before heading into the shower.

"The floors are a little slippery from the slurry of dust and water. Be careful," Brooks warned him, moving to the side so Rogan could step under the showerhead. The swirl of water over the tiles turned black immediately.

"Ugh! Now I really want to get clean," Rogan said.

"Let me help." Brooks grabbed some soap and spread it over Rogan's back. His fingers lingered on his mate's skin longer than necessary, much to Rogan's appreciation.

"That feels good," Rogan encouraged.

"Face me now. I'll get your chest," Brooks requested.

Rogan faced him, allowing his adventurous mate free rein. Brooks's hands lingered on his shoulders and on the ridges in his abdomen. How far would he go? Rogan could see Brooks's body responding to the contact as quickly as his own did. Rogan held his breath as his mate smoothed the soap lower.

When his hand closed around Rogan's erection, Rogan groaned in delight. "I crave your touch. More, Adventurer. Stroke me harder." Rogan wrapped his hand around Brooks's and showed him what he enjoyed the most. "Yes. Like that."

When he battled to stay in control, Rogan gently tugged

Brooks's hand away. "You'll make me come. I would rather spill inside you."

Even under the residual dust streaking Brooks's face, Rogan saw his mate blush. More telling was the jerk of his cock against Rogan's thigh. He grabbed some soap, eager to get his hands on his mate. "It's your turn."

After thoroughly washing his mate's grimy face, Rogan took care of his own. He kissed his mate, fueling the growing ardor between them. Rogan loved the man's taste. He was addictive. Tangling his tongue with Brooks, Rogan challenged him and celebrated when his mate responded eagerly.

While keen to enjoy the temptation his mate provided, Rogan forced himself to back up slightly. "I need to get you clean first. I'll start with your hair and work down."

Pouring shampoo on Brooks's scalp, he massaged the suds through the silky brown hair. It was a bit shaggy and uneven. "We need to ask Lalani to trim your hair."

"I did it myself last time. I can hack it off."

"Are you okay with Lalani cutting it? She enjoys pampering people," Rogan asked.

"Sure. I just don't want to bother her."

"I'll check before I schedule anything," Rogan promised. "Now, lean back and let me rinse away the shampoo."

With that finished, he moved on to Brooks' chest. Stroking soap over his skin, Rogan felt a raised, rough patch on Brooks's skin a second before he heard his mate hiss in distress. Rogan turned him into the water, rinsing his skin clean.

"That stung," Brooks explained. "Sorry."

"Don't apologize. I think you're having a reaction. Could these be hives all over your skin?"

"Yeah, probably. I've gotten them in the past. I'm allergic to dust."

"Why didn't you tell me?" Rogan demanded. He couldn't

Rogan

believe his mate hadn't told him about this. Instantly both guilty and concerned, he scanned Brooks's skin to assess the extent of the problem.

"I wanted to help. It's okay. I'll take an allergy pill, and it will be better."

"Do you have any of those pills?"

"Maybe I forgot to grab them?"

Rogan shook his head. His mate was going to be in such trouble after they got this handled. First, he had to remove the rest of the dust. "This is going to sting. I'll use the gentlest soap I have."

"I'm fine. Don't worry."

Right. Rogan sent a message to his horde, asking for one of the dragons to find a doctor as he washed his mate quickly. He stood under the spray before finishing his own shower and shampoo. Drake answered immediately that he was in the city center and would bring someone quickly.

As he ushered Brooks out of the shower, his mate pointed to the tube of lubricant now balanced on the shower railing. "Aren't we going to...?"

"First medicine, then pleasure," Rogan answered as he patted his mate's skin dry. The welts were getting bigger.

"This is worse than I've had it before. Can we go to my grandma's house for my meds?"

"The doctor is coming."

"Really? By horse? You're probably faster."

Rogan could tell his mate was worried. His breathing was becoming raspy.

We're here.

Drake's message pushed back Rogan's growing concern. He answered quickly, *On our way!*

Rogan grabbed a towel and wrapped Brooks inside before scooping him up and racing toward the front of the mansion.

His staff was already on alert from the gold dragon landing outside. His housekeeper held the door open.

"Doctor. Thank you for coming," Rogan told him as he ran forward. "My mate is having an allergic reaction and doesn't have his tablets."

The doctor took one look at Brooks as Rogan set him on his feet in front of him. He grabbed his bag, saying, "It's good you called for help. Pills aren't going to treat this." He quickly drew a shot.

"This is best in his buttocks," the doctor said.

Rogan turned Brooks around and whipped the towel to the side to expose his bottom.

"Hey!" Brooks protested before adding, "Ouch!" as the doctor administered the shot.

"You're okay, Brooks," Rogan assured him, before asking the doctor, "How long will we have to wait until it helps?"

"It should be fast. We should see the hives fade as the medicine works. Brooks, I'm going to listen to your lungs. I don't like the sound of your breathing."

"I'm okay," Brooks rasped.

"Let the doctor check you out, Adventurer," Rogan told him.

A few minutes later, the doctor plucked the earpieces away and slung the instrument around his shoulders. "We'll give that medicine a bit of time to act. It will make Brooks extremely tired for the next twelve to twenty-four hours. How is the itch, young man?"

"I think it's better," Brooks said.

"Your voice is improving. That worried me," the doctor admitted before noting, "The redness is starting to fade. I believe he's on the mend."

Rogan felt some of the tension ease. Humans were so fragile. He couldn't lose Brooks now. Rogan tenderly smoothed Brooks's hair from his forehead.

Brooks swayed, and Rogan immediately pulled him to his side to steady him. "Will he need any more treatment?"

"I'll leave some pills for him. We could benefit from restocking some essential medical supplies before everything is exhausted," the doctor suggested. "The pharmacists have inventoried all the supplies around Wyvern. They could give you a list of in-demand drugs."

"Good idea. I'll touch base with them tomorrow," Drake promised, stepping forward to handle that request. "When you're ready, Doctor, I'll take you back."

"My kids are going to be so envious of me. I appreciate you making me a superstar in their eyes," the doctor joked.

"Thank you for coming, Doctor," Rogan said.

"My pleasure. Mates are important. Here are some pills. The shot will work for the next twelve hours. If Brooks still has hives, give him a pill every four hours until they disappear. He should go to bed. Make him rest. Push fluids."

"I will follow your directions," Rogan said, accepting the pills.

"Dust caused this?" the doctor asked.

"Yes."

"Mitigate that as much as possible," the doctor directed.

Rogan nodded. He understood this was his fault. It would be a long time before he forgave himself for endangering his mate. "Thank you again, doctor. I owe you. Your family may call on me when you require assistance."

The doctor appeared moved by this invaluable promise. "Thank you, Rogan. My congratulations on finding your mate. This will only be one thing you discover about each other."

Rogan grasped that the learned man acknowledged this

was simply an unfortunate event and not Rogan's fault. He nodded to thank the doctor before facing the gold dragon.

Drake, I also owe you.

You would do the same for me. Take care of your mate. Aurora and I look forward to spending time with you both soon.

Soon, Rogan promised, whisking his yawning mate up into his arms. He turned and carried him into the mansion. There was a special room waiting for Brooks that he hadn't seen yet.

Chapter 7

Dragging himself from the extreme drowsiness clouding his mind, Brooks glanced around the room. He didn't remember being in here. He reached out and closed his hand around the bars of the railing extending around the comfortable bed. The resulting rattle brought Rogan to his side.

"Brooks. You look less foggy." Rogan's voice sounded pleased.

Flashes of his mate bathing his itchy patches with cool liquid, cuddling him to his chest, and rocking him flooded his mind as Rogan slid the railing down that contained him. He struggled to push himself to a seated position.

"You are not yet at full strength, Adventurer. Let me help you," Rogan said as he scooped him off the supportive mattress.

Brooks wrapped his arms around his mate's neck and held on as Rogan walked to a large chair. When Rogan sat down, the chair glided underneath them. Propped up in Rogan's arms, Brooks studied the room.

"What is this place?"

"It's your playroom. You thrashed around when the hives got itchy. You were safer in your crib. Here, drink."

Rogan placed a bottle at his lips, and automatically, Brooks sucked. A thick creamy mixture filled his mouth, and he hummed in delight as it soothed his dry throat. It took several minutes for him to realize he was drinking from a bottle like an infant. Immediately, he pushed Rogan's hand away and struggled to get up.

"Whoa, Adventurer. You're okay," Rogan reassured him as he helped him sit up.

That small rebellion completely wiped out his energy. Still, he forced himself to protest, "I'm not a baby."

"Mate, that medicine knocked you for a loop. This bottle got nutrition inside you without a mess so you could recover to this point. Your hives are almost completely gone. Soon, you won't need any more."

"I can stop now," Brooks argued.

"Not going to happen. We will follow the doctor's instructions. Come. Stretch out and drink. You need liquids to recover."

Rogan gently helped him back into position and held the bottle to his lips. Brooks was too thirsty to refuse. He devoured it.

"Good job, Mate. We've avoided this discussion for too long."

Brooks met his gaze, and a shiver ran down his spine. His mate's eyes seemed to see into his soul.

"All my previous mates dreamed of a secret lifestyle. One I am also wired to lead. I thought perhaps you were the exception, and that was fine. Each mate is a special individual."

Rogan paused to brush Brooks's hair from his forehead. "I found your stuffie, Brooks. Can you share with me what his name is?"

His heart raced. Rogan seemed to understand—to see deep inside him. Brooks shook his head, trying to buy himself time to think. Maybe he could excuse keeping the stuffie by saying it was a childhood memento... He didn't want to do that to Rogue. The plush dragon meant too much.

"It's okay, Adventurer. There shouldn't be secrets between mates. If you can't don't wish to say it aloud, there's another way. Would you like to try that?"

Not sure what he suggested, Brooks shrugged.

"I understand. Close your eyes, Brooks."

Rogan waited until his mate followed his directions. Brooks heard him shift slightly, then Rogan's fingers pressed to his forehead. "Concentrate here for a minute. My touch is your anchor. When you're ready, mentally turn your attention, putting the touch of my hand directly behind you."

When Brooks looked up to meet Rogan's gaze, his mate reassured him. "It may sound impossible, but we can do this together. You must keep your eyes closed for this adventure. Can you be brave?"

Brooks slammed his eyelids shut as Rogan tugged the bottle from his mouth. Instantly, he could concentrate more. Resolve filled him. Whatever happened, he trusted his mate. He focused on the warmth of Rogan's hand and slowly turned to peer into his mind. Overwhelmed by the sight that appeared in front of him, Brooks backed up to brace himself against Rogan's touch.

"That's it. Good job. Look around a bit. Can you see all the colors zipping past? I want you to search for a red line. It will shoot past several times before you can focus on it and pin the light in front of you."

Brooks caught a glimpse of crimson to his left. Then another on his right. Determined, he mentally jumped on the next one and saw it stretch in front of him.

"That's it, Brooks. You're doing so well. Trace that line as far as necessary until you find a door."

Zigging and zagging, Brooks slid his attention along the red line. It was tricky in several places, and he struggled to continue. Finally, a huge wooden door rose before him. Three locks spanned the front with the red line piercing the center.

"Yes. Brooks, you're there. Write your name on the door with your finger. That is your door."

Brooks pressed a fingertip to the wooden surface. Solid and slightly weathered, the surface featured a dot now where he'd tapped it. Slowly, he stretched out the letters. On impulse, he added Rogan's name and drew a heart around it.

"So sweet, Brooks. I love that." Rogan's voice sounded emotional. Brooks almost opened his eyes to check on his mate but controlled that desire.

As if he'd followed Brooks's thoughts, Rogan rubbed his forehead. "Stay steady, Adventurer. You're almost there. The first lock is open. That happened when we consummated our union. I want you to unfasten the second lock."

Brooks shifted his hand away from the door and grabbed the lock. He hesitated, debating whether or not this was wise. Rogan said nothing, just held him close as he sent gentle support through their connection. Trusting his mate, Brooks powered the stubborn lock open.

Instantly, their bond intensified. Brooks opened his eyes as Rogan's emotions and desire for Brooks flooded into him. "You love me."

"I do, Brooks. I love every part of you, inside and out."

Images of Rogan caring for him over the last few days flooded Brooks's mind. He could also sense his mate's enjoyment of tending to him intimately. Brooks's fantasies of submitting to someone had always seemed impossible. Could he have that type of relationship with Rogan? Could he be that brave? Brooks gathered his courage.

"Rogue," he blurted.

"Ah, so close to my name. I will thank your stuffie for guarding you before I could find you."

"My mom always said I wouldn't leave the store without the red dragon. It's the only stuffie I ever wanted," Brooks shared before whispering, "I can feel you so much more."

And we can talk easily in any form. Try it.

You can hear me?

Loud and clear, Little boy.

You know I'm Little? I haven't admitted that to anyone.

And I suspect you would have hidden that from me as well.

Brooks nodded. Concealing that part of him had been a priority. He had thought no one would understand. *What made you suspect?*

You called me Daddy. I would love it if you'd use that name for me.

Brooks forced himself to be brave. He didn't want to hide anymore. He was safe with Rogan. *Daddy, I love you too.*

Rogan pulled him into his arms, hugging him tight. *Thank you for being brave, Brooks.*

Pressing his lips to Rogan's, Brooks kissed him with all the emotions tumbling around inside him and froze, as he could sense how Rogan enjoyed the kiss as well.

It's okay, Brooks. Our connection is stronger.

Rogan ran a caressing hand down Brooks's side to squeeze his bottom. Instantly, his cock hardened in response. It was as if that open lock magnified everything. What would sex be like now? He kissed Rogan and clung to his shoulders as the sensations overwhelmed him. How would it feel when Rogan slid into him?

Better than you can imagine.

Rogan lifted his head. "You are not recovered enough for those activities, Adventurer. One more day of medicine should erase the last of the hives and then we will find out. Finish your milk."

When Rogan placed the nipple at his lips, Brooks shot him an unhappy stare and drank. The chair glided underneath him, soothing his frustration. By the time he finished the last of the liquid inside, Brooks struggled to keep his eyes open. Rogan lifted him and placed him gently in bed before covering him with a fluffy comforter.

When soft fabric brushed his cheek, Brooks reached out an arm to loop around his cherished stuffie, pulling it close. His Daddy rubbed his back until he drifted to sleep.

Chapter 8

Holding his Little on his lap, Rogan could sense the mating bond was easing. His prediction had come true, and the last of Brooks's hives had disappeared overnight. Without the medicine to make him drowsy, his mate had recovered his energy.

To his delight, Brooks had chosen to play in his nursery today. After his last mate had passed, Rogan had gutted the previous nursery and turned it into a guest bedroom. This special area would only be Brooks's. The games and activities he'd gathered while he searched for a mate were a big hit.

"I like that this is my room," Brooks said softly.

"I do too."

"Could you tell me about your other mates?"

"Of course. I've had five other mates—four female and one male."

"Who was your first?"

"Ian McDougall. A strapping man of Scottish descent. I don't know who was more surprised, his family or Ian. He struggled in having his life's course totally upended. Dedicated to his family, he chose not to run away from Wyvern, but I'm sure he wanted to a million times. Until his heart wouldn't allow him to hide our bond."

"You said that almost all mates are Little?"

"I won't reveal any living person's secrets, Brooks, but I shared accurate statistics with you," Rogan answered honestly.

"So, let's go back to the past. Your other mates were women?"

"Yes. Three from other families and another from the MacDougall clan."

"No other Battlefields?" Brooks asked.

"No, Adventurer. You are my first from that family." Rogan loved Brooks's proud smile. "They will carve your name in the risers of the steps on the square soon. We should go check out the other mates memorialized there."

"Is there a mate you've loved over the others?"

Rogan had expected a question like this. "Love is a wonderful thing. It is infinite, without limitations. I care deeply about each of my mates and miss them now that they are gone. After a mourning period each time, the hurt of losing them fades, and only wonderful memories remain. I would never choose to not have had them in my life. The love I shared with each mate makes me eager to experience the happiness a bond provides again. And I look forward to the uniqueness each mate brings to my life."

"That makes sense. I think it would be sad to know you'll outlive a mate," Brooks suggested.

"It is. But the world has many surprises up its sleeves. While my dragon is a fierce beast who can vanquish foes, I am not eternal. At some point, old age, disease, or a lucky blow could end me."

When Brooks appeared worried, Rogan added, "I do not expect any of those to happen in the next few centuries. Dragons usually live for eons."

"Good. Would you take me for a flight?"

"Of course. Go back to our room and grab your sneakers," Rogan directed. Brooks obviously needed a break from the serious conversation.

His mate ran out the door and disappeared before he could remind Brooks to stay close. To his relief, no shout of pain echoed down the hall. As Rogan suspected, their connection had matured. The mate bond now allowed Brooks more freedom. No longer did they need to stay in extremely close proximity.

Brooks burst into the room, holding one sneaker with the other untied on his foot. "Hey, I had one shoe on when I realized that didn't hurt!"

"Come here, Brooks. Let me tie your laces and help with the other."

Brooks climbed back on Rogan's lap and let him get Brooks straightened out. Rogan kissed the side of his neck. "I think our bond has decided you need some freedom. Don't push it too hard. I always want to know where you are."

"Yes, Daddy."

"Want me to ask if Lalani can cut your hair? We could zip over there," Rogan suggested, ruffling Brooks's hair.

"I'd love that. I'm having trouble seeing. Or you could loan me a pair of scissors?"

"Not happening. Let me see if Lalani is working today."

By the time they were outside and Rogan had shifted, Khadar had responded with an invitation to visit. *We're on our way, Adventurer.*

Brooks responded with happy thoughts and fireworks that filled Rogan's mind, making him snort amused smoke, to the delight of his mate. Rogan had a feeling his unique mate would come up with many novel ways to surprise him.

In a few minutes, Brooks settled in place and held on

firmly. The desperate hold of a newbie had eased. Brooks trusted him.

Let's go, Adventurer!

Can I see your mountain?

Of course.

Rogan flew on each side of the rocky peak, highlighting the most breathtaking spots in his territory. His mate's awe and enjoyment of the tour radiated into Rogan's mind. He could see it for the first time through Brooks's eyes. Rogan was proud of his land and was glad to get to soar once again in the crisp, clean air without fear of an attack.

During the age of technology, the horde had hunted mainly at night and had only frequented Wyvern in human form. The knowledge of their existence had fallen to the Guardians of each family's pact and was passed on when the end of their lives was imminent. In the high-tech era, who would believe that dragons existed?

Almost as if Brooks could read his mind, his mate asked, *What would have happened if something hadn't taken out our computers and machines?*

I can't answer that, Brooks. Perhaps the end of dragons?

No. Dragons will always exist.

Perhaps you are right. Look! Lalani is waving to you. Shall I wave back?

Yes, Daddy!

Rogan tilted back and forth, waggling his wings at Lalani below and giving his mate a wild ride as well.

"Wooohoooo!" Brooks hooted into the air as he clung to Rogan's neck. Gone was his apprehension about flying. He loved soaring through the air with his Daddy.

That was fun! One more time!

Hold on, Adventurer. I'm landing.

After settling on the ground and shifting, Rogan guided

Rogan

Brooks forward to meet Khadar and Lalani. "Greetings. Thank you for allowing us to visit."

"My mate enjoys having others around," Khadar answered. Rogan nodded. He understood completely. Dragons were not the most social of creatures.

"Daddy, be nice. Hi, Brooks! Hi, Rogan. How are you both?" Lalani asked with a twinkle in her eye.

"Good," Brooks answered with a grin that Rogan was pleased to note. It appeared Brooks had begun to acclimate to his life as a dragon's mate. Lalani's gentle teasing didn't make him uncomfortable.

"Can you trim up this shaggy guy? I can barely see his eyes," Rogan said.

"Of course. Come to my salon. I always set up under that gigantic tree," Lalani said and pointed a short distance away. "Your Daddy... Um, Rogan can come with us if you need to be close to him."

"Go try it, Brooks," Rogan urged, wanting Brooks to have a chance to ask questions or chat without a dragon around.

"I should be fine," Brooks answered. "I ran to get my shoes today and discovered it didn't hurt."

"That's great and sad." Lalani's voice drifted to the dragons as she led Brooks away. "I enjoy sticking close to Khadar. It was nice to have a built-in excuse."

"How's your mate adjusting?" Khadar asked as he led the way up to the covered porch equipped with chairs.

"Well. It's been quite an adjustment for him," Rogan admitted and settled into a seat before changing the subject. "Can you catch me up on what's happened during the bonding?"

"Keres states he doesn't remember attacking you and your mate. We're going to have to deal with him soon, I'm afraid."

"That's not a good sign. Do we have many original Wyverns returning these days?" Rogan asked.

"No. The founding families report that all living relatives are now inside the borders. Drake and the Guardians are organizing another social in hopes of Keres finding his elusive mate."

"If she or he is around. Keres may have missed his mate in this generation." Both men shook their heads unhappily at this suggestion,

"That would be the worst-case scenario," Khadar admitted. Their gazes meshed in sorrow. For a dragon who was at the end of their ability to survive without a mate, it was more than that. It was a death sentence. "Are the others talking about driving him away?"

"So far, we're avoiding that conversation. It will have to be discussed soon."

Rogan shook his head. Several hundred years ago, he'd been in Keres's situation. Struggling to hold on to his sanity while maintaining his faith in finding a mate. A small twinkle of existence had popped into his mind in his darkest moments. He'd grabbed that light like it was the northern star and maintained hope. A mate's life force began. Eighteen years later, he visited every birthday celebration until he'd found her.

The horde sympathized with Keres, but they also had to protect their mates. They would not allow the black dragon to hurt or terrorize them.

"Any news on the smoke?" Rogan asked, changing the subject.

"Nothing. I'd like to believe we knocked back their operations when we decimated that storage area," Khadar stated.

"But you don't."

"No. They're biding their time. An attack has followed each mating."

"You expect another now," Rogan guessed.

"Yes. If I'm right, it will be soon. I've upped my patrols. I hate to admit I'd gotten lazy from using cameras and sensors from the past."

"And the chatter on social media. Some people can't keep their plans to themselves," Rogan said, shaking his head.

A housekeeper emerged from Khadar's mansion with a tray. The green dragon leapt to his feet and took the heavy item from her before setting it on a table. "Thank you, Louise. We'll wait to dive in until our mates join us. Could you bring us two beers from my stash?"

"Of course, Khadar."

With all the factories and breweries closed, the previously manufactured beverages were in limited supply. "We have a group of men working on relearning the way to brew a large quantity of beer efficiently without the help of technology," Khadar stated when they both had bottles in their hands and had sampled the concoction inside.

"Beer? No way." Brooks jogged to Rogan's side and started to climb up on his lap. He caught himself and stepped away.

"Come back, Mate. I'll share." Rogan held out his bottle and scooped Brooks up. Sitting his mate on his lap, he patted Brooks's thigh. He was proud of his handsome mate and rushed to reassure him. *You are fine, Adventurer. We are with friends.*

Aloud, he said, "Let me see. Do I even recognize the mate stealing my beer?"

Brooks grinned at him and turned his head in each direction to show off Lalani's talent. "You look different, Rogan, now that I can see you."

"Rascal," Rogan growled before looking at the hairdresser. "Thank you, Lalani."

"I'm glad to help. I noticed that one section of Brooks's bangs is becoming red at the roots." She leaned forward to peer closely at Rogan. "It's exactly where your streak is. How is that happening to Brooks?"

"I had one mate in the past who had a pink section appear in her blonde hair after we'd been together for several years. Perhaps it's just contact with my magnetic personality," Rogan joked. Brooks tensed at the reminder he'd had other mates, making Rogan wish he could erase those words. Brooks had wanted to be the only one who looked like him.

"Can that even be possible? Have you always had that red flourish?" Lalani asked in fascination.

"I don't ever remember not having it. If you look at that spot on my dragon form, you'll discover there are a few black scales in the same place."

From the fascination blooming in Brooks and Lalani's eyes, they couldn't wait to check for that. He took the opportunity to rectify his earlier mistake. "My bond with the mate with the pink streak was the strongest I'd ever experienced until Brooks came along and blew that to smithereens." He was glad to see the corners of Brooks's mouth flex upward.

"That's fascinating," Lalani said. "Brooks's is going to be deep red—like yours, Rogan."

"You'll be twins," Khadar stated nonchalantly.

Lalani glanced back and forth between Rogan and Brooks. He was massively muscular while Brooks was lean and fit. She covered her mouth as she tried to hold in the laughter that threatened at her mate's suggestion.

"I think it's better if we don't suggest we're siblings," Rogan recommended.

That statement pushed Lalani over the edge. Her giggles were infectious, and soon everyone joined in. Rogan rejoiced in his mate's relaxed enjoyment. It appeared Brooks was adjusting well to his new life.

A few minutes later, Lalani said, "I have to go to the bathroom. Brooks, would you like to come in with me and use the facilities? Maybe check out my room?"

"Yes, please."

🐪 🐪 🐪

Brooks waited in the hallway for Lalani to return. Checking out his surroundings, he spotted precious paintings and other pieces of art lining the massive passage. Was that...?

Brooks walked closer to look at a portrait of Khadar. Dressed in old-fashioned clothing, he looked almost exactly the same as in the present day. How old was that painting?

"He's very regal, isn't he?" Lalani asked. "He said his eyes changed once while he was posing, and the artist was terrified of him forever."

"That's awesome. I wonder if he did that on purpose."

"I never thought of that. I'm going to ask tonight. My area is through that doorway. It's kind of babyish. Is that okay?"

"Of course. It's great you have a space for yourself," Brooks commented.

"They're pretty overwhelming, aren't they? The dragons, I mean."

"Definitely. Can you imagine being Skye with two?" Brooks asked.

"No way. She's happy, though. I mean really, really happy. It's great she has them to take care of her. Here's my room." Lalani led the way into a beautiful room. "We could play a board game or put a puzzle together."

"That sounds fun. This is a beautiful space, Lalani." Brooks glanced around, noting the oversized furniture like he had in his room. He spotted a worn dragon stuffie in the crib. "Is that yours?"

"It is. It's so funny. All the new mates have one. Hey, wait. Do you?"

"Rogue. He's a red dragon. My folks bought him when I wouldn't leave the store without him."

Lalani nodded knowingly. "That fits with the stories from the other mates. I was adopted, but my birth mom sent Lettuce with me."

Brooks turned to the stuffie and shook its paw. "Nice to meet you, Lettuce. I'll bring Rogue next time and introduce the two of you."

"We should have a tea party with our stuffies. We could invite everyone." The excitement on Lalani's face faded, and she quickly added, "Maybe boys don't like tea parties."

"Offer me cookies and I'll put on a tiara," Brooks assured her.

"Oh, fun. Sorry. We've been girls for so long...."

"Lalani, I understand it's weird that Rogan's mate is a guy. It's outside my normal as well. I'd like to get to know the other mates better. From what I understand, we're going to be around for a while. Friends are going to be important."

"Exactly. Daddy and I started this puzzle. Want to work on it with me?"

"Will he mind?"

"Not at all. Khadar is bad at puzzles," Lalani shared.

"Really? You'd think he'd be used to looking down at things."

Brooks and Lalani worked quietly on the puzzle for a few minutes. Finally, Brooks asked the question rolling around in his head. "Does everyone call their mate Daddy?"

"Yes." She was quiet as they worked on the puzzle for a few minutes before she met his gaze and asked, "How about you?"

He hadn't blushed for years, but his face heated, and he suspected he was red. "Sometimes."

Rogan

"It gets easier. You know, the more time you're together."

Brooks nodded and focused on the puzzle for a few minutes before saying, "Thanks."

"You're welcome, Brooks. You can ask me anything. I'll probably answer," she joked.

He smiled. Everything was going to be okay. He wasn't alone. He had Rogan and the other mates. It seemed like they understood each other.

Chapter 9

Looking across the dinner table at Rogan, Brooks studied his handsome mate. "What's the difference between dragons? I mean, is there something special about a black dragon that doesn't apply to a red one or is it like hair color for humans? Some of you have green scales and other blue ones?"

"It's a bit more complicated than that, Adventurer. Each color denotes special talents. We do not divulge these facts with all humans, for information contains power. As my mate, I will trust you not to share this insight with others," Rogan told him solemnly.

"Of course. I wouldn't tell anyone about your secret abilities," Brooks promised.

"Thank you, Mate. While dragons range in strength, the colors tell certain facts. For example, a black dragon has the most fire resistance, while a bronze dragon can absorb more electricity."

"And a red dragon?"

"Red dragons are the fastest."

"Of course you are—like the best high-performance vehicles. Who wants a gray Corvette?" Brooks joked.

"Indeed. Red is superior."

"Are you always the same color as your parents?" This conversation fascinated Brooks.

"Female dragons are rare. They alone can create a new dragon. The hatchling's hue will reflect its talents," Rogan explained.

"So a fast baby will be red?"

"Exactly."

"What color were your parents?" Brooks asked.

"My sire is a blue dragon. He doesn't answer questions about the female dragon who laid my egg. To do so would endanger her. Males raise the dragon unless they're at the end of their lifespan. Then usually another male from the sire's horde steps in to protect the deceased member's replacement until it is able to survive on its own."

"Your father is alive?"

"I believe he is. The connection between us is still strong. When it disappears, I will know he is gone," Rogan explained.

"And the connection with your mother?"

"It doesn't exist."

"Because that would put her at peril?" Brooks guessed.

"Exactly. So would you like to go racing around today on your sports-dragon?" Rogan asked with a smile.

"Yes!" Brooks couldn't ever imagine turning down the opportunity to ride on his mate's back. He'd never considered skydiving or paragliding, but seeing everything from above while the wind whipped through his hair was exciting.

Setting his fork on his plate, Brooks suggested, "Let's go."

"Three more bites, Adventurer. Then I will take you."

Rolling his eyes at the dragon shifter's bossiness, Brooks wolfed down the rest of his breakfast. He didn't want to get hungry as they zipped around. Somehow Rogan always sensed how he felt. His mate would end their fun early if his stomach growled.

Twenty minutes later, he scrambled up Rogan's scales to his reserved spot. It got easier each time.

Soon you'll be a pro.

It's weird to have you eavesdrop on my thoughts.

You can guard them from me if you would like, but I only pick up on those with high emotion.

Like celebrations?

And if you are frightened or unhappy. Those things I wish to know.

Okay. Brooks could understand that. If he was scared of something, maybe he wanted a big, bad, super-fast dragon to pick up on that.

Rogan didn't comment for several seconds, allowing him to make up his mind. Brooks liked that the dragon answered his questions, and while Rogan had a lot of rules that all seemed to endanger Brooks's butt, when Brooks thought about them, they made sense.

Thank you, Mate.

You're welcome. That doesn't mean my mind is an open book you can rifle through.

I promise you, Brooks. I will only pry when there is danger. Now, do you see that mountain on the horizon? The one with the ring of clouds around it?

That's miles away!

How long do you think it will take to get there?

The entire day? Brooks guessed.

Try thirty minutes.

No way!

Hold on tight! Rogan ordered. As soon as Brooks's arms squeezed tightly around his neck, he raced toward the high peak.

"Rogan!" Brooks shouted into the air. "Wooohooooo!" This was the absolute best!

When Rogan landed, Brooks slid from his spot. His legs felt wobbly underneath him, like they had when he'd visited an amusement park as a kid.

Dragons are superior to any roller coaster, Rogan informed him snootily.

"I think I'm okay going slow for a while. Maybe save light speed for emergencies?"

Good idea, Brooks. Let me change, and we'll go have some lunch. Sara suggested we have a picnic lunch on the back lawn.

Standing away to allow his mate to shift into human form, Brooks considered whether his stomach could handle food. The resulting hungry growl answered that question. The cook was amazing.

"I heard that. Let's go see what she's got for us. I could devour a cow or two." Rogan held out his hand for Brooks's.

Intertwining his fingers with his mate's, Brooks asked, "Really?"

Rogan laughed before answering, "I can only eat a full cow when I'm in dragon form. However, the roast beef sandwiches are all mine."

"Hey, I like roast beef!"

"I promise to share if I get kisses." Rogan tugged Brooks close and wrapped his arms around Brooks's waist.

Offering his lips to Rogan, Brooks returned the hug as his mate's mouth captured his. Instant fire ignited between them. Brooks didn't understand the potent desire between them. He simply knew he craved Rogan's touch.

Maybe we could delay lunch? Brooks suggested when he could gather his thoughts.

Rogan lifted Brooks easily over his shoulder and stalked toward the tall hedges at the beginning of the garden maze. "Let's play hide and seek, Mate. I'll give you a thirty-second head start. Go!"

Frozen, Brooks looked at him in astonishment.

"You've wasted five seconds, Mate."

Catching on, Brooks raced off at high speed. He raced through the maze, trying to put as much distance between himself and Rogan as possible. After the promised delay, thundering footsteps followed him. Brooks increased his pace.

He burst into the open center of the maze and spun in a circle, attempting to figure out which path to take. Brooks strained his ears, trying to hear where Rogan was. Silence echoed around him. His cock strained against his zipper. He wanted whatever Rogan had in mind.

Brooks chose a random opening and ran toward it. He reached it as Rogan stepped into the clearing. Before he could turn, Rogan grabbed the belt loops on his jeans, controlling Brooks.

"Mine," the shifter growled as his eyes flashed red. He held Brooks securely in place with one hand as his other unfastened his mate's jeans and pushed them to the ground.

Rogan dropped to his knees in front of Brooks and leaned in to lick his mate's shaft from base to tip before meeting Brooks's gaze. "Let's see how fast I can make you come."

When his mate's mouth closed around his cock, Brooks's eyes rolled up into his head. He wouldn't last long.

Chapter 10

Glancing across his study, Rogan smiled at the sight of Brooks in a leather chair, engrossed in a book. His mate had found the bookshelf with mysteries and thrillers from the past and present and dived in. Managing his estate still took several hours a week. Rogan had delayed attending to things while Brooks settled into his new life.

"Finish that chapter, Adventurer, and we'll go into town." The dragons had set up a rotation where they dropped in to help at the square. Rescue missions had ended at this point. The dragons had either found those Wyverns caught outside the town by the tech failure, or they had returned by their own power.

"Can I go see my grandmother?"

"Of course. She'd love to visit with you."

A short time later, Brooks climbed onto Rogan's back. Even in dragon form, Rogan loved the hug that Brooks delivered to his neck as he settled into position. His mate... Rogan couldn't sum up how much he cared for Brooks. Love didn't seem to encompass all the feelings inside him.

Stop being a sappy dragon.

Daddy? I missed that message.

Sorry, Adventurer. That was me thinking too hard. I want to remember to talk to my herd master when we get to my estate.

I'll remind you.

Thank you, Brooks. I need to land at the square. Are you okay walking to your grandmother's house? He didn't want to let Brooks out of his sight, but realized it was important for his mate to do normal things.

Of course. I don't think the big bad wolf is going to be at grandma's house.

If he is, punch him in the nose and get out of there.

Got it. Punch and run.

Rogan hovered over the square. Alerted by the beat of his wings, the crowd looked up and automatically parted to create a landing zone. He settled onto the ground. Immediately, several community leaders approached. He could tell they had something to discuss. This might take longer than he thought.

Brooks, call me if you need me. I may be tied up for a while.

I will. No rush. And oooh! Tying you up sounds good.

You're tempting me, Adventurer.

Brooks's answering grin told him he knew exactly what he was doing.

Rogan shifted before his mate, aroused by him too much. The crowd did not need to see an erect dragon.

"Rogan! We're glad to see you. Could you help us melt scrap metal to create some tools? We could use your fire."

"Of course. Show me what you're doing first," he requested and checked to make sure Brooks had set off. Rogan saw him turn the corner and disappear.

A movement to his right caught his attention. The alleyway was empty. On a hunch, he excused himself and headed for the passage. No one. Rogan walked between the buildings, checking for hiding spots or doorways.

Behind a dumpster, he spotted a small panel that was slightly ajar. He shoved the large metal bin out of the way. Sensing the heat through the wall, he guessed a person lurked inside. "Come out," he roared.

No one answered. *Of course not.*

"If I have to come get you, that doesn't bode well for you," he growled.

The panel moved slightly, and a young female voice asked, "You won't eat me?"

"No."

Seconds ticked by. The gap widened, and a young teenager dressed in an overcoat stepped out with a hand stuffed in her pocket. "What do you want, dragon?" The fear in her eyes erased the bravado in her words.

It was way too hot to merit a coat. "Tell me your name." He memorized her appearance—matted brown hair, blue eyes, hollow cheeks, and a slight form. She hadn't been eating regularly.

"Puddintane. Ask me again and I'll tell you the same."

He noticed she angled herself away from him to distract him from her hidden hand. "It is not wise to mess with dragons," Rogan reminded her with a steely stare. "Tell me your name."

The teenager swallowed hard and admitted, "May."

"Thank you, May. Now, pull that hand slowly out of your pocket."

"I'd rather not."

"Why?"

"Please don't make me," she whispered.

He could tell she wavered between two choices. "May, what is your family name? Do you need help?"

She shook her head frantically. "No. I'm fine."

"Tell me what's going on."

"No."

"Then I'll have no choice but to take you to people who will help figure this out," Rogan explained.

"I don't want to do this."

He was already on guard, now looking at the distress on her face, his concern skyrocketed—for them both. "You have to talk to me, May. Maybe we can figure this out together."

"I'm not one of them. I like dragons."

"Is someone forcing you to do something against dragons, May?" Rogan asked. Who did she refer to? Could this be the same people who had attacked them before?

She nodded. "If I don't, they'll hurt my brother."

"We need to avoid that. Is anyone watching us?"

"They're inside the building. Where it's safe. They can't see." She spat out the words in disgust. They'd sent a kid to do a job they were too scared to do themselves.

"Where's your brother? Is he in the building too?"

"No. They took him away. He's only three."

Anyone near the square? Rogan sent to the horde. *I have a problem here.*

And I thought you were a big, tough dragon.

Keres. Of course. Rogan mentally shook his head. He'd have to rely on the black dragon. *Fair warning. I believe I have someone that's involved with the attacks on dragons.*

"May, I promise you I'm going to protect you and your brother. Can you tell me if you have powder in your pocket?" Rogan asked, refocusing quickly on the teenager.

"I don't know. That's what it might be. They gave me a packet and told me to throw it at you."

"Did they inform you it would kill you as well?"

She stared at him hard. "Are you telling me the truth?"

"Dragons don't lie, May."

"Will you rescue my brother?"

"I promise I will try. First, I need to help you. Pull your hand out of your pocket."

"If I do, the dust will fly."

Rogan debated quickly. In this small alleyway, the effects of the powder would affect May and himself. It was best to handle this here.

"Want me to take her out?" Keres growled from behind Rogan.

"What?" May cried, dodging behind the dumpster.

"Keres. Stay at the mouth of the alley. Keep everyone out," Rogan directed as he maintained his focus on the young woman.

"May. That's Keres. He's an ass who always says the wrong thing. He won't hurt you."

"Promise?"

"I won't let anyone hurt you, May."

To Rogan's relief, May stepped out from behind the dumpster to face him once again.

"Let's get that coat off you. Slide your arm out of the sleeve."

May slowly followed his directions. Soon the coat dangled from one shoulder. It was way too big. Maybe there would be enough material to encapsulate her hand to trap the chemicals in the fabric instead of releasing them into the air.

"I'm going to come closer and wrap the coat around your hand. Then you're going to pull your fist out slowly. How did they get your fingers in this?" Rogan asked to give her something else to focus on. She was already stiff with fear. He wound the coat tightly around her wrist.

"They'd already stuffed a bag in the pocket when they put it on me. They made me put on a glove and then slide my fingers into the container. I was supposed to grab a handful, or the whole packet, and throw it at you."

"You're too close, Rogan," Keres called.

Rogan waved him off. *Tell me something I don't know. There's no other way to do this.*

"Okay, at the count of five, I'm going to pull this away from you. Keep your fingers straight. Once your hand is free from the pocket, wiggle your fingers around to wipe off any powder."

Brooks. I have a situation here. Stay where you are. I'm taking care of it. I love you, Adventurer.

"One. Two."

Daddy?

"Three. Four."

I love you!

"Five."

Rogan whisked off the coat and stared at the strips coated with powder attached to the glove. They'd added double-stick tape to make sure she pulled out some of the lethal substance. He ripped the glove off and dropped it. Grabbing May's arm, he ran toward Keres.

Gray tinged the edges of his vision, and Rogan lost his orientation as everything whirled chaotically. Pushing May in front of him as he fell, Rogan called, "Take her, Keres."

Daddy!

Chapter 11

Please let him be okay.

Brooks studied the still figure stretched out in his bed. He reached forward to brush his hair from his eyes. His fingers lingered on that red streak.

He has to be okay.

After the first message, Brooks had jumped to his feet and raced for the square. The seven blocks that separated him from his mate seemed miles long as he ran as fast as possible. He found Keres holding a limp figure, with Drake in dragon form spitting fire into the alleyway. Drake had blocked him from running to Rogan.

When Drake stopped the flames, Rogan hadn't moved. They'd brought him to his mansion, hoping for the best. Brooks guessed from both Keres's and Drake's faces, they didn't think he'd recover.

Daddy? Can you hear me?

Brooks tried communicating through their connection for the millionth time. Rogan didn't answer.

Struggling to hold on to hope, Brooks dropped his forehead

onto Rogan's hand, resting limp on the covers. He had to get better.

Sending all the love he had in his heart through their connection, Brooks tried to convince himself that he could still feel Rogan's life force. There was something there, but that spark felt so weak. Brooks's stomach churned with fear and anxiety. How could his strong, fierce Daddy be so affected by a simple powder?

The press of Rogan's hand against his skin reminded him of the tour through his head. That door. Three locks secured it. His connection with Rogan had strengthened when he'd opened that second lock. What would happen if he unlocked the third? He'd never asked.

Could he find his way back to the door? He had to try.

Brooks focused on Rogan's hand pressing against his forehead. He followed the steps Rogan had coached him through. When he faced the darkness of his mind, Brooks searched for the red illuminated line. It darted here and there, eluding him. Stubbornly, he focused.

There!

He traced the light to his door. The sight of the heart with his and Rogan's names made his eyes water. Brooks ignored his tears. He could cry later. He reached forward to that third lock.

Expecting it would be as tough to rotate as the second was, Brooks powered it open. A rush of sensations flooded him as the lever turned easily. Suddenly, he had access to Rogan's mind.

Nausea welled up inside him as absolute dizziness struck him. How was Rogan surviving this? Brooks had no idea which way was up. He tightened his fingers on the soft covers on their bed. That tethered him slightly, slowing down the spin of the images swirling around him.

Brooks?

Daddy. I'm here. Help me find you.

Get out of my mind, Brooks. It's too dangerous for you.

I'm not going anywhere.

It took every ounce of his concentration, but Brooks searched for something to assist him. A red flash appeared on the fringe of his sight. Before he could lock in on it, the light was gone, but now he had a plan. He ignored the topsy-turviness around him and tried to spot it again.

The third time, he had the red streak fixed in front of him. Wading through the chaos streaming around him, Brooks ignored everything except that glowing line. With each step he took, Rogan's presence grew stronger.

Daddy. I'm coming. Look for me.

Brooks, the longer you remain in here, the harder it will be for you to escape. Go now, mate. I love you.

To hell with that. You've fought this long. Fucking swim through this nightmare to meet me. Come now, Daddy.

I'm going to spank you so hard.

And I'm going to hold you to that promise, Daddy.

His energy faded each second he existed in this disorderly space. The whirling memories and information inside Rogan's brain tempted Brooks to lose track of the path he followed. Brooks pushed away his curiosity and put one foot in front of the other.

Frightful creatures beset him. All dark and shadowy with gnashing teeth and sharp nails, they looked like escapees from horrible science experiments. Most kept their distance, but as he got closer, Brooks had to dodge a few and chanced losing his connection with Rogan. He didn't know if they would or could hurt him, but he wouldn't risk it.

Brooks reached a section of a deep valley between steep

cliffs. Once inside, the smooth rock faces would pin him inside like a trap. He debated. Scale the mountains or go through that dangerous trail through the darkness? He chose the quicker path through the valley. Climbing over the mountains would take too long. His energy wouldn't last.

Entering the dark passage, Brooks didn't glance left or right to spot anything lurking to harm him. A twisted hand reached out and viciously swiped at his arm, slicing the skin open. Blood welled from the wounds and rolled down his arm. Red droplets soaked into the dirt. He jogged forward, wasting his dwindling energy to get away from whatever that was. Brooks ripped his T-shirt down the center of his chest and wrapped the material around his biceps.

An ear-shattering roar sounded above him. Brooks sped up into a run. The edge of cliffs loomed in front of him. A rush of wind ruffled his hair. Talons raked over his back, and he threw himself into the dirt and shouted. For the first time, Brooks doubted he'd reach Rogan. Out of the edges of his fixed gaze, he spotted familiar red scales.

Daddy! Call off your dragon.

He's not listening to me. Get out of here, Brooks!

The desperation in Rogan's voice sent bone-chilling fear through him. He pushed himself up to his feet and pelted forward. Rogan's presence filled his senses. Brooks could feel and smell him ahead. His Daddy was close.

The dangerous sound of flapping wings sounded above him. He had to make it a few more feet. The temperature rose around him. The dragon inhaled. Flames would follow.

I love you, Daddy.

Red light flared around Brooks, obliterating his vision. He squeezed his eyelids closed as he continued his forward progress and slammed into an immovable object. *Daddy, I'm not going to make it.*

Rogan

I've got you, Brooks. A powerful arm wrapped around his waist, pulling him against a rock-solid chest.

Brooks forced his eyes open. *Daddy!*

Relief burst over him as Brooks realized Rogan had him. Brooks peeked above them to take in a red glowing dome extending around them. Rogan projected the barrier from the hand he held over their heads.

Somehow with that flickering shield, Rogan guarded them from the dragon's fire. Brooks could feel Rogan pulling the dragon toward him. Rogan needed to reconnect himself with his beast. In the tumult, the dragon shifter had lost the other half of his essence.

Brooks could see the dragon hesitate. He had to be attracted by the red light of the protective shield. The fierce creature landed and paced forward. Pressed against his Daddy, Brooks hugged him tighter as Rogan began to shake from the effort to reunite with the rampaging beast. Brooks funneled the last of his energy through their mate bond, and Rogan drew on it to steady himself.

"Come on. Just a bit closer," Rogan commanded, his voice strong and convincing.

Taking one more step forward, the dragon's snout touched the projected light. Red sparks flew in all directions around them like a breathtaking firework explosion. Brooks buried his head against the crook of Rogan's neck as his mate's other arm wrapped securely around him.

You did it, Adventurer. Rest now.

The last of Brooks' energy drained from his body, and blackness filled him as he crumpled.

Brooks snuggled closer to the hard chest he slept on. He blinked his eyes as his mind burst into alertness. Pushing himself up on a forearm, he studied his mate. Rogan slept peacefully. Gone was the torment that had floated across his features.

Gently dropping his head to Rogan's chest, Brooks celebrated. He suspected his mate would never have escaped from that nightmarish environment without him opening that third lock. Brooks couldn't imagine how his mate had survived with the two distinct parts of his psyche split apart. Had the powder done that to him?

"You're thinking very hard, Mate," Rogan's voice interrupted his wandering mind.

"Rogan. I thought I'd lost you," Brooks told him, trying to hold all the emotions inside him at seeing his mate's blue eyes staring back at him.

"I owe you a serious spanking. Luckily for your bottom, I need food and water first."

"Do you have enough energy to go hunting?"

"Yes. Run to ask Sara to send word to isolate a half dozen cows in the rear pasture while we get dressed."

Rogan had never taken him when he'd eaten in dragon form. "I'm going this time?"

"I can't be away from you. And my dragon demands your closeness," Rogan told him.

"Um... I'm not sure I want to see the beast that attacked me."

"That's why he wants to see you," Rogan told him.

Brooks nodded. He wouldn't argue with Rogan this soon after almost losing him.

"Should you let the horde know you're okay? Someone came every day to check on you."

"They felt me wake up but aren't intruding on us now. Where's May?"

"She's staying with my grandmother."

"I owe Elenore my thanks. May requires our help," Rogan shared, sitting up. "Food first. Dragons and May next. Spanking and burying myself in your bottom after that."

A wave of heated desire filled Brooks's mind. Instantly, he was harder than steel. "Whoa!"

"You're going to want to close that third lock, Adventurer. There is no buffer at the moment between our minds." Rogan stood and stroked over his own hard shaft.

Brooks struggled to keep his eyes from rolling back in his head. "Daddy," he whispered.

"Perhaps there's one thing I need to do before you flip that lock closed, Adventurer."

Rogan dropped to his knees at the edge of the bed and pulled Brooks close. Grabbing the elastic band of the borrowed sweatpants Brooks wore, he ripped them down the front.

"Those were yours!"

Passion filled Rogan's eyes, taking Brooks's breath away. Who cared about pants? He leaned back to watch as Rogan wrapped his powerful hand around Brooks's now exposed shaft. Arousal overwhelmed him. He could feel everything Rogan did.

Rogan slowly lowered his head to wrap his lips around his cock. Liquid warmth surrounded him, making Brooks groan. The reciprocal taste of his own skin filled his mind simultaneously. His cock spurted a small amount of fluid, giving him a taste of his own come as Rogan hummed in delight.

"This is mind-blowing," he whispered, and Rogan intensified his pull on Brooks's erection. A deep groan tumbled from Brooks's lips as his fingers curled into the covers below him.

Just wait...

With that mental message, Rogan swirled his tongue along the sensitive length of Brooks's cock. Brooks shook his head, already struggling for control. He didn't want this to end. Not yet.

Rogan slid a hand up Brooks's thigh to cradle his balls in a gentle grip that contrasted with the power contained in the dragon shifter's grip. When Rogan tugged, Brooks thrust his hips up toward his mate, driving his shaft into the warmth of Rogan's mouth.

"Sorry, sorry, sorry," Brooks chanted, not sure how much Rogan could handle.

Amusement filled Brooks's mind. Pleasure dashed that away as Rogan swallowed. Brooks had never experienced anything like this. Rogan pushed his arousal hard, raising and lowering his mouth around Brooks's cock. When Rogan's finger strayed to press on that small sensitive area between his sac and his puckered opening, Brooks lost it.

"Fuck!" Brooks shouted into the room as he exploded into the heat of Rogan's mouth.

When his mate released his cock and sat up to meet his gaze intimately as he licked his lips, Brooks's mind was too shattered to talk. He shook his head at Rogan in disbelief.

Rogan smiled and gathered Brooks to hold him tightly until he recovered.

"That's dangerous," Brooks whispered.

"Thank you for thinking of deepening our connection. Torn apart from my dragon, I wouldn't have escaped from my mind," Rogan admitted.

"Whatever that powder is, we need to stop them," Brooks told him.

"We will. First, close the lock?" Rogan asked.

When Brooks nodded, Rogan continued, "Then, food.

Let's go get dressed, and we'll alert the household that you rescued me. That is, if they didn't hear you," Rogan teased.

Brooks stuck out his tongue at his mate as his face heated. He'd blushed more in the last month than he remembered in his teen years. And he loved every minute of their time together.

Chapter 12

Rogan waited calmly in his dragon form as his mate advanced hesitantly toward him. He radiated reassurance to Brooks. He'd already stressed to Brooks that the separation from his human side had driven the dragon to react like an animal instead of a sentient being. While Brooks seemed to understand, he still acted jumpy around the dragon. Finally, Brooks stood in front of him.

"Good dragon," Brooks soothed.

He needs your touch.

Brooks reached out a hand to stroke his nose and jumped away when Rogan pressed his snout into the caress. "Whoops. You liked that," Brooks said, stepping forward again to repeat the gesture. This time, when Rogan nudged him, Brooks laughed and moved closer.

"You weren't trying to hurt me, were you?" Brooks asked.

Rogan shook his massive head and gently bumped his chest with his snout. When Brooks shifted forward, he wrapped his arms around the beast's neck. Treasuring the hug, Rogan rested his head against Brooks's spine, squeezing him back.

Are you okay, Mate?

Yes. Let's go flying.

Brooks raced to his forelegs and clambered up to sit in his normal spot. Once his mate settled securely into place, Rogan launched himself into the air. Heading directly to the rear pasture, Rogan flew low to scoop up a cow before rising into the clouds to devour his meal.

Steak, hamburger, roast. Steak, hamburger, roast.

Rogan chuckled at the words running on repeat in his mate's mind as Brooks struggled to handle the sound of snapping bones as the dragon devoured the creature. *She was gone before her hooves left the ground. The cow didn't suffer.*

Thanks for sharing that tidbit of information... Steak, hamburger, roast. Steak, hamburger, roast.

Restocking his resources, Rogan ate the bare minimum of two more cows before heading to Drake's, where the dragons gathered. He'd avoid serving beef for dinner for a few nights.

By the time they'd reached the rendezvous point, Brooks had stopped chanting. He leaned forward to peer over Rogan's head. *A lot of dragons are down there. Do you think Keres is coherent today?*

If he has a focus, he's fine. Keres will concentrate on the threat to the dragons.

Okay.

Rogan understood the hesitancy in his mate's tone. He wished he could erase his mate's apprehension about the black dragon. It was impossible since even he wasn't sure how firm a grasp Keres had on reality. So far, Keres had supported the horde when they'd needed him.

I will never let him touch you, Adventurer. He would have to go through me.

I'm not afraid of him.

Stay close to me, Adventurer. Let's not tempt him.

With that, Rogan landed near the gathering below. His

mate scrambled off and stood on the far side of Rogan. When he'd shifted, Rogan reached out a hand for his mate's and led him forward to meet everyone.

Immediately, the other mates rushed forward to greet Brooks. Skye was the first to hug him—her usual aversion to physical contact obviously overwhelmed by her joy in seeing him.

"Hi, Skye. Everything's okay now," Brooks reassured her.

"We were all scared. When Oldrik got hit by that powder, he said it was awful. He couldn't detect which way was up or down," Skye told him as she stepped back to allow Lalani, Aurora, and Ciel to greet him as well.

"My direct hit had a more severe effect. It ripped my dragon and human sides apart," Rogan shared.

Shocked silence followed that announcement.

Drake shook his head. "How did you survive that?"

"My mate opened the third lock and came searching through my mind for me," Rogan said.

"That's ballsy," Keres drawled. "Perhaps I should focus on finding a male mate too."

"A perfect mate will show up for you," Skye assured him. The blue and bronze dragons' mate had a special relationship with Keres. The black dragon had returned her, Derek, and Brooks to Wyvern. Keres favored the quiet woman, to her mates' consternation. The two had a special bond.

"Thank you, Skye. Let's hope that happens before the horde forces me away," Keres said pointedly, staring at the assembled dragons.

"Keres. Did you get any information from May?" Rogan interrupted the conversational jab before it could continue.

"Not much. The powder completely knocked her out. Luckily, I pushed the air drifting over the two of you with my wings and blasted the coat and glove you removed from her with minimal burning," Keres told them.

"We'll need to talk to her. She followed their directions because the bad guys were holding her younger brother hostage," Rogan said.

"Those jerks. Who would do that to a little boy?" Lalani asked.

"Zealots," Drake suggested. "Did you pick up any clues about what's inspiring these attacks, Rogan?"

"Not anything we haven't considered. We do have another link to them. That's more than we had last week. May might be able to help us. I can lead us to the building they were in. I'm sure they're cleared out by now, but we could pick up some clues there," Rogan shared.

"They'll have booby-trapped that house. It's too dangerous to go in. We'll have to destroy it." Argenis vetoed any exploration.

"You're right," Rogan agreed. "So, shall we start with May?"

"As soon as she wakes up," Khadar suggested. "In the meantime, we need to do something. The bad guys got May and her brother from somewhere. Someone may be looking for two kids."

"I doubt relatives will come forward. May is too thin. My guess is no one has cared for her for a long time," Rogan told them.

"We could check at the orphanage or with the official who handles foster care children?" Lalani guessed.

"That's a possibility. Let's put out the word for any information about them. Wyverns will be concerned about two children being used as bait and held to blackmail a minor," Ardon stated firmly.

Rogan

"I'll go with Brooks to his grandmother's to check on May," Rogan volunteered.

"We'll go check with the Guardians in the square." Ardon spoke for Oldrik and Skye.

"I'm going to walk the perimeter of that building," Keres announced. When the others turned to stare at him in concern, he promised, "I'll be careful."

"The two of us will touch base with the school administration and religious leaders. One of them may have insight about the missing children," Khadar pointed to himself and Argenis.

"Let your mates ask questions as well. Sometimes, humans will chat with other fragile humans instead of dragons," Keres suggested.

The horde members nodded. Each shifter with a mate knew their loved ones would jump at an opportunity to help the kids in this situation. The dragon shifters would enlist all the help they could get. Their unknown attackers were becoming more desperate.

🐉🐉🐉

"Hi, Grandmother." Brooks greeted Elenore warmly before giving her a hug.

"Brooks. You look happy. I'm glad you're adjusting to your new life so well. And Rogan! I was so worried about you. The other dragons seemed hesitant to say when you'd feel better," Elenore shared.

"My recovery is thanks to your grandson. I would have lost my way without him. How's May?" Rogan asked.

"Rogan? Did you find my brother?"

"May! You're awake. I bet you're hungry. Everyone's in the kitchen." Elenore tried to shoo the group to the table, but May didn't move. She stared at Rogan, waiting for him to respond.

"That powder got me as well, May. I just woke up and came over here to see if you could give me some details. The other dragons and their mates are checking everywhere to get information about you and your brother. Let's go sit down and you can answer some questions for me. Anything you can provide might help."

She seemed reluctant, but May nodded and followed Elenore. The kindly grandmother set apples in front of the humans and then started gathering more to serve. May immediately took a huge bite from the apple. She ate like she was starving as Elenore put things in front of her—not turning her nose up at anything.

Brooks? Does your grandmother keep paper and pen around? I'd like to write things down.

Still munching on his apple, Brooks nodded as he stood. He walked a short distance away and opened a drawer in the desk at the edge of the kitchen to pull out a pad and ballpoint. He waved them at his grandmother to signal to her they were borrowing them. Rogan spotted a picture sitting on the desk and was struck again by how much Brooks resembled his father.

Rogan glanced back at Elenore and spotted a bit of his handsome mate in her as well. Maybe it was the determined set of her jaw. That trend of stubbornness seemed to run in the family, much to the detriment of Brooks's butt.

"Thank you, Elenore. It will be easier for us all to disperse information with it written down," Rogan said. He appreciated Elenore more each time they met.

"Good idea," Elenore said with a nod.

"May, what's your brother's name?" Rogan asked, refocusing on the teenager at the table.

"Edwin Cesar. He's three. His fourth birthday will be on Sept 16th," May answered.

"Describe him for me," Rogan requested.

"He's goofy. Cute with dark hair and dark eyes. Medium skin tone," she told them.

"How tall? Thin? Chubby?" Rogan pursued details to help them. "Do you have a picture of him?"

"Mom did on her phone, but that doesn't function anymore. He comes up to my hip. Over three feet. He's thin. We haven't had a lot to eat since Mom died."

"Did something happen to her during the change?" Brooks asked.

"No. She passed away about a month earlier. From cancer. She made me promise to take Edwin to his father. We were on our way through Wyvern when everything happened."

"You said his father. You two have the same mother but different fathers?" Brooks clarified, trying to put the pieces together correctly.

"Mom couldn't tell me who my father was. She knew Edwin's because he moved her in for a while, and she stopped working. He was killed stealing a car when Edwin was two. Mom went back to the streets. We lived in that house for a while, but his father's family booted us out and sold that place."

"Where were you from, May?" Rogan asked.

"I'm not really from anywhere. When we were homeless, we looked for a place with a roof where we might find some food and stayed there until it was too dangerous. Then we moved on," May reported.

"May, I've been saving this package of cookies for the right time. Let's open them up," Elenore suggested, sitting down at the now laden table. She removed the wrapper and pulled out a plastic tray of soft chocolate chip cookies. "Everyone, help yourself."

Brooks took the first one to break the ice as May hesitated.

"Oh, these are good. I'm going to miss treats like this when there are no more around."

May helped herself to a cookie and nibbled at it as if stretching out the pleasure of eating it. Finally, she looked up and said, "It's going to be hard to locate my brother. They obviously knew I'd be dead if I followed your instructions. They may be out of town by now."

"Oh, they're still in town. They want to be close to the dragons, and no one is getting in now without a tie to Wyvern. Anyone they've got on the inside is going to hang around. We just need to find them," Rogan said, taking a cookie. He ate one bite and nodded. "Yummy," he remarked before handing the rest to Brooks to finish.

"Could we save a couple for Edwin? You know, if we find him?" May asked quietly.

"Silly me! We should have kept the whole package for the celebration *when* the dragons find him," Elenore said, jumping back to her feet. "I have a few plastic bags with zippers. I'll seal it in that for us to eat later."

Hope filled May's eyes. They had to locate her brother.

Rogan sent the description out to the dragons as they met with the community leaders. Perhaps that would assist. The odds were low that anything would help. Finding and eliminating these recreants became more important every day.

Chapter 13

Hey! Can anyone come flame me? Keres requested through the horde's communication connection.

I'm on my way, Drake replied, without asking questions.

What's going on, Keres? Rogan demanded.

A hazmat suit fell into my possession, so I explored that building, Keres explained. *If Drake can blast me from a distance, I'll be able to remove it without harming myself or him. And, as a bonus, we can use it again.*

A hazmat suit? Rogan repeated in amazement. His mind battled between amazement at Keres's creativity in coming up with this solution to getting inside with a semblance of safety and his exasperation that Keres had done exactly what the horde had decided not to do.

Seemed like it might be handy someday.

Did you find anything, Keres? Drake asked.

Lots. Come join me, and I'll show you, Keres invited.

Rogan quickly filled in Brooks before adding, "I'm not taking you with me, Adventurer—just in case there's a risk of contamination."

"If anyone is low on life force, it's you," Brooks suggested.

"I'll stay behind. I'm not doing that again."

"Keep me informed?" Brooks asked.

"You bet. Give me a kiss and I'll be off."

When he got there, Rogan discovered the other dragons had chosen not to bring their mates either. No one trusted the black dragon. Drake had already torched Keres. The black dragon had draped the now-steaming protective suit over a bush to cool down. Keres's plan seemed to have worked without exposing him to the powder.

"Oldrik thought of flapping our wings to send any smoke into the building," Ardon explained as Keres walked forward.

"So, the place was booby-trapped. I was covered by the dust five times. Thank goodness for the suit. It kept the toxic mixture away. The bad guys weren't taking chances that someone could avoid running into it. I managed to get a look at a map left on the table. Bringing it out without transporting the toxins with it posed a challenge, so I stood and studied it. Here." Keres sent a mental image through their link.

"That seems suspicious to lead us to their newest hideout," Argenis said.

"Definitely. But it's the only major clue I found. Other than a large collection number of one specific brand of tools," Keres said. "I paid attention when I noticed the same logo. Does anyone have a clue where they sell Snap-On wrenches and screwdrivers?"

"Ask the mates. They will know," Drake suggested.

The dragons all fell quiet. A few minutes later, Khadar reported, "Lalani says her mother's neighbor had a Snap-On tool truck parked in the driveway."

"Luckily, I dropped Aurora off at her parents' house. Her dad reports Wyvern didn't have a Snap-On store. Dealers distributed it to mechanics directly," Drake reported.

"Why do I guess the truck was where the Petersons lived?"

Ardon asked. The dragons had banished that family for targeting a mate.

"It has to be close at least. Maybe on the other side of Lalani's mother's house?" Khadar suggested. "I don't remember spotting one there when I was dealing with them."

"It could have been moved to bring the tools closer to the labor area after the change," Drake suggested. "I shifted a bunch of trailers for the workers when they consolidated things together into a tool library. I don't remember it, but maybe?"

"So, it could be something in the neighbors' places or in the new location," Rogan said. "Keres? You up to wearing that suit again?"

"Tomorrow would be better. It's scorching hot still. I don't want it to melt on my skin and drive away my future mate," the black dragon joked.

"Good idea," Argenis said. "I'll fly over the gathered supplies to check if the truck is there now and report back. The supervisors will have a log of whether we went there. Someone should check out the place on the map—or at least go peek from a distance as if we were gathering intel."

"I'll see to that," Khadar volunteered. "I'll botch blending in with the green trees so they see me. They'll think I'm hiding."

"Everyone, come to my estate for dinner tonight. The mates will be happy together, and we can talk about what Argenis and Khadar find. We can create a plan that we'll all follow," Oldrik suggested with a pointed glance at Keres.

"Hey, it was my risk to take," Keres declared. The horde considered that and then agreed.

With their plans made, the shifters divided up, eager to contact their mates. Rogan suspected their humans would be almost as anxious as Brooks was now. He glanced meaningfully at Keres. *No vigilante action tonight by yourself, hmmm?*

Keres answered. *Going insane, remember? I'll try to coordinate with the horde the next I dive into the enemies' lair.*

Rogan knew the odds of that happening were slim. He shook his head and shifted. Time to get back to Brooks.

🐉🐉🐉

"And he went in without telling anyone? What if he'd gotten trapped like you did?" Brooks demanded.

"It's possible we could have tracked him there," Rogan said with a shrug.

"And then been in danger from the traps he set off in his fancy suit!"

Rogan created an image in his mind of Keres dressed in a black velvet tuxedo with white fur around the lapels and cuffs. Rogan added a fuzzy hat as an extra embellishment and snorted. Brooks rolled his eyes at his mate, but a good portion of his anger at the black dragon dissipated.

"I believe Keres is giving up. He was trying to help in his own way," Rogan said gently.

"I know."

A wave of sadness spread through Brooks. Rogan could have faced the same fate as Keres. Had Brooks not met Drake and then Skye, he might have abandoned his trek to Wyvern. Or someone could have killed him along the route. People outside of Wyvern had lost their minds when nothing worked, and the authorities were no longer in control.

Warm arms wrapped around Brooks and pulled him close. "Don't think about what might have happened, Brooks. We found each other," Rogan reminded him.

"That makes everything better," Brooks agreed with a smile.

"It does. Now, I have something important to take care of," Rogan reminded him.

"What?"

"Your spanking."

"You're not scaring me. You've threatened that before and nothing," Brooks said with a laugh. The serious expression on Rogan's face that followed the statement skyrocketed his concern.

"My apologies, Brooks. I've misled you to think I wouldn't follow through. Obviously, I've allowed outside events to interfere with our relationship and your adjustment to your new life. I will spank you today and promise there will be more in the future."

Rogan stalked forward with unmistakable determination written on his face. Brooks froze, considering whether to flee or fight. He was torn between dread and excitement at the thought of the taste of pain his mate would ensure he experienced. Rogan reached him before he could decide and threw him over his broad shoulder. The air gusted out of Brooks's lungs, preventing him from speaking as Rogan headed for the nursery.

Stop it! Brooks frantically told his body as his cock twitched in excitement. *This isn't good. You don't want this.*

By the time he regained his breath, Rogan had set him back on his feet in front of the large rocking chair. His Daddy unfastened the button at the top of his jeans and pulled the zipper down as Brooks twisted helplessly. "Wait! Why are you spanking me?"

"I told you to get out of my mind after I found May." Rogan dragged his jeans and knit boxers to his calves.

"But without me, you wouldn't have escaped. You said that yourself," Brooks pointed out, as cool air swirled over his exposed skin. Brooks pushed futilely against the dragon shifter's powerful chest, hoping to get away before his response was too apparent.

"That doesn't make what you did less dangerous. Nor does it erase the fact that you did not do as I instructed. What if we hadn't escaped together?"

"That was my decision to make!"

Rogan lifted him effortlessly and draped Brooks over his rock-hard thighs. "Your choice ended the moment I told you to flee. You need to follow my directions without question from now on. This punishment will reinforce that lesson."

Before Brooks could argue, Rogan's heavy hand landed on his butt. Hard. "Ouch! Stop that!" Brooks howled as the swats continued. He knew it was a miniscule amount of Rogan's strength, but the heat and sting built on his skin. Brooks kicked his feet, trying to free himself. Rogan simply anchored Brooks's flailing limbs with his leg, holding him solidly in place.

Brooks tried hitting Rogan's calf in front of his face, but that hurt his hand more than it probably did Rogan. He was as solid as stone. Out of escape options, Brooks started to tear up. Brooks never cried. He didn't show weakness.

"Stop! Fuck you," Brooks rallied, upset by his emotions. The next swat on his bottom set his skin on fire. Brooks was unable to stop them, and tears poured down his cheeks. Sobs poured from his mouth, and he drooped unresisting over Rogan's lap.

Immediately, Rogan switched from spanking to soothing. He rubbed his hand over Brooks's heated flesh. "You have to let someone else take care of things now, Adventurer. I'm glad you're strong and fearless, but I need you to allow me to keep you safe. Without you, I'm nothing."

"You're a fucking dragon. You're everything!" Brooks sobbed. No one else would have gotten by with spanking him.

"You don't get it, Brooks." Rogan gathered Brooks in his

arms and turned him to cradle his mate on his lap. He kissed him softly as he wiped his tears away. "You are my life force. If you had been trapped in my mind with me, I would have spent an eternity tormented by your death. I don't matter. Only you do."

Brooks shook his head. "That's not true. You're more vital than me. You're a dragon."

"A dragon who will not exist without a human match. You are my mate. If I die and you survive, only the horde will miss me. If you pass, your entire lineage suffers. I made a pact with your forefather. Dragons must live up to their word."

"Is that like the law?" Brooks blustered.

"Yes. I exist to protect my mate. It is my purpose. My reason for being. You must allow me to fulfill my destiny."

"I'm never going to think I'm more important than you are," Brooks said stubbornly.

"Then you remember this spanking. We'll repeat it as many times as necessary to convince you," Rogan told him.

"Dragons beat their mates?" Brooks challenged.

"Punish, yes. Beat, no. Does anything other than your bottom hurt? And your pride?" Rogan asked, making him focus.

"My butt hurts enough for my whole body," Brooks snapped. He deliberately didn't address the pride aspect. That was obvious.

Rogan stroked a finger along his erection. *Crap! He had noticed.*

"Mates enjoy their dragon's touch. They also realize there are rewards for accepting discipline and learning how to adjust to their new role in life." Rogan lifted his hand to his mouth and licked his palm and fingers. He deliberately wrapped his wet grip around Brooks's cock. "This wasn't a fight, mate. This was a Daddy teaching his Little."

Brooks searched Rogan's face, checking for something negative—a sneer, a laugh, a smirk. All he found was love and concern. That hand pulled the length of his shaft from root to tip, sending shock waves through him. The sting of his spanking lingered and blended with the thrill of sensation of his Daddy's hands on him.

A spurt of excitement welled from his cock. Using his slightly rough thumb, Rogan spread that fluid over the velvety tip of Brooks's erection. A groan tumbled from Brooks's mouth. That combination of sensations overloaded his brain, pushing his arousal higher than he'd ever experienced before.

"Daddys make decisions for their mates. They show their love by fulfilling secret desires and needs. I can sense what you would enjoy, Brooks. I know you," Rogan told him in that deep, rough voice that always sent shivers of passion through him.

Brooks debated. He could argue, or he could admit that Rogan had him completely figured out. Choosing a third option, Brooks begged, "Stroke me more."

Rogan's slow wink told Brooks his response revealed everything to his Daddy. "You've got it, Adventurer."

Brooks's apprehension lessened. Rogan wouldn't make him bare his soul completely now.

Rogan pulled a tube of lubricant from the drawer of the table next to the rocker. The snap of the cap opening sounded like a gunshot in the quiet nursery. Brooks reminded himself to breathe as Rogan squeezed some onto his palm. He hesitated for a few seconds, allowing the slick gel to warm slightly on his fingers before spreading it over Brooks's shaft.

This time, his fist slid smoothly around Brooks's erection. Brooks closed his eyes to concentrate on the sensation but needed to see Rogan caressing him. Peeking under his lashes, he forced himself to focus on that moving hand. Damn. He wouldn't last long.

Rogan squeezed a bit harder before loosening his grip to

glide along the length of Brooks's erection. Heat built as he quickened his motion. Brooks pushed his pelvis into that fist as the stimulation decimated his control. Each brush of Rogan's rough denim jeans against his punished bottom reminded him of the spanking his Daddy had delivered. Breathing heavily, Brooks bit his lip, trying to distract himself. He didn't want this delicious torture to end.

"Come, Adventurer. I have other plans for your red bottom," Rogan whispered softly against his ear.

With a shout, Brooks emptied himself into that tight fist.

Chapter 14

Brooks tried to pull himself together on the flight to Oldrik's mansion. His Daddy had held him and Rogue close until the last moment when they needed to take a shower and get dressed to go. Brooks hoped no one could tell by the stiff way he walked that he'd gotten a spanking followed by intense love-making. Being the only guy was hard. The women mates couldn't understand.

He looked normal when they'd left. All the tear marks were gone, and his jeans covered the lingering pink blush on his butt. Just remembering that spanking made him hot again. *Stop it. Down!* Brooks hoped his shaft would listen this time.

"No one will know, Adventurer. And if they figure it out, they'll understand more than you anticipate. Remember you were going to ask if the other mates had any hobbies to see if you had some fun things in common."

"You suggested that before. I don't think I'll try to wiggle my way into any activities they've already set up. That seems pushy."

"Totally up to you," Rogan assured him as he settled on the ground.

Brooks rolled his eyes as he slid to the grass. Rogan was going to ask the other dragons. "Fine, I'll check if the subject comes up."

"Perfect. Have fun."

Brooks could feel Rogan's gaze on him as he walked to the group of mates who chatted with each other. He obviously hadn't hidden his nervousness well. Brooks did appreciate the stream of support that flooded toward him through their connection.

"Hi!" Brooks greeted the others and gritted his teeth when his voice sounded a bit too cheerful to be natural.

"Brooks! We're glad to see you. We were talking about getting together to read the book Ciel is writing," Aurora shared, seemingly not noticing Brooks' tension.

"Brooks might not like to read Daddy books," Ciel blurted as she turned a delightful shade of pink.

Instantly intrigued, Brooks guessed from her blush that the book was spicy at least. Daddy books. Was that a thing? "I don't believe I've ever read a Daddy book. Are they a relationship like we have with our mates?" Brooks asked, forcing himself to ask the question. He mentally crossed his fingers, hoping he hadn't read the others wrong.

"Yes. That's what makes them so delicious," Lalani said with a grin. "It turns out all the girls had found these books before we discovered what Wyvern had in store for us. Surprise! Fated dragon Daddies."

The group laughed at that term. Almost everyone's lips moved as they repeated that phrase to themselves. There was no doubt the shifters would be called that from now on. Fated dragon Daddies.

"I think of it as training and orientation," Ciel joked. "Daddy and I devoured the few paperbacks we each had in that genre together. When we ran out, he suggested I try writing my own."

"What? On an old manual typewriter?" Brooks asked in disbelief.

"Exactly. I'm getting better. I don't get the keys jammed together much anymore. Aurora read each chapter after I finished it. Now the audience has grown to the four of us—well, five if you are interested. You don't have to join if you aren't interested," Ciel assured him quickly.

"Count me in. Is there a chance we could go back to chapter one so I can hear the beginning too?" Brooks asked. He couldn't believe this was a thing and couldn't wait.

"Of course. We usually start at the beginning. That helps everyone remember the story," Lalani said. When even her darker skin tone turned red, Brooks knew those stories were spicy to say the least.

"Each mate takes a chapter," Ciel told him.

"Count me in. I can't wait. When's the next reading?" Brooks asked.

"I finished a chapter last night before bed. We could review it today," Ciel admitted. "We need to find a quiet spot. The Daddies enjoy eavesdropping and getting ideas."

When each mate in the group nodded almost as one, Brooks suspected this had happened more than once. Ciel must be creative. "After dinner?"

"Yes. My nursery." Skye shared the gathering spot.

"You haven't been in there yet, I bet." Aurora helped him. "I'll signal you, and we can sneak off together. That way I can show you where it is."

Brooks nodded. He couldn't wait. Glancing over at Rogan, he found the dragon shifter studying him. His Daddy had to be aware of this and had suggested Brooks ask about activities to break the ice. How crafty of him. Brooks sent him a thumbs-up signal to let Rogan know he was fine and saw his Daddy smile in response before turning back to talk to the others.

After eating three of the hot dogs Oldrik's amazing chef had created from scratch, along with homemade chips and ice cream, Brooks followed Aurora into the darkened mansion.

"That was an incredible dinner. Who knew stuff made at home tastes so much better than the packaged stuff I used to buy at the grocery store?" Brooks said to Aurora.

"We are very lucky to have our mates' staffs. In town, all of Wyvern is banding together to assist each other. A lot of neighborhoods have communal dinners where everyone contributes. The dragons help by collecting supplies we can't make here in Wyvern. Sugar is the one I'm going to miss, but medicine is scary."

"I'd thought of that," Brooks commented. His grandmother had run out of her high blood pressure medicine a month ago. The dragons checked in different pharmacies on their scouting trips, but the manufactured supplies were running low. It was a scary time to have a health condition or illness.

His grandmother didn't seem too concerned. She tried to eat right and exercise—which she'd always done in the past as well. Brooks hated to imagine a future without her. That's why he'd stayed in one place for so long after returning this time to Wyvern. Having time with her meant a lot to him.

As he turned into Skye's nursery, sad thoughts blew out of his mind. The room was so her. The high ceiling and enormous windows would make this a perfect art space for her creations. Already, Skye had drawn dragons on the longest wall, using the door in the design to make it blend in beautifully. He guessed this space connected to her Daddies' rooms on each side while giving her some quiet space.

Arriving last, Brooks quickly took a seat on the floor next to Skye. He inadvertently let out a groan as he settled on his spanked bottom. Catching himself, Brooks scanned the room, hoping the others hadn't noticed.

Everyone smiled at him. Brooks shifted to jump to his feet to flee. Skye put a hand on his knee and pointed around the circle. Three women raised their hand.

"Join the club," she told him cryptically.

"What club?" he asked, not wishing to jump to a conclusion.

"The 'we made bad choices, and our Daddies spanked us' club," Lalani admitted. "We all winced or moaned as we sat down. It's a dead giveaway for everyone else. Skye needs pillows."

"Next time," Skye promised and made an X over her heart.

"Okay. Let's move to the story. I hope you like this new chapter I wrote last week. I was inspired after recovering from a cold. Daddy had warned me it was too chilly to swim in his pond, but I insisted," Ciel admitted.

"Oh," Aurora said, waggling her eyebrows. "Our Daddies have a huge assortment of old-fashioned medical tools they collected years ago."

Brooks tried to unpack the implications that statement had included in it as the others nodded in agreement. He really wanted to ask what type of equipment their dragon shifters had, but maybe he didn't want to find out.

"Let Brooks listen to the first chapters. He hasn't heard the story yet," Lalani suggested as Ciel started passing out the chapters.

He got the sixth chapter and forced himself to turn it upside down on the floor so he didn't get distracted while the others read. By the time Ciel was halfway through the first chapter, he stretched out on his stomach. Others chose to follow his example. He guessed it wasn't for the same reason since they didn't need to hide their arousal, but it was more comfortable for his butt too.

Ciel was really talented. He enjoyed the story. The sixth chapter was sweet, to his relief. Reading the steamy stuff might have challenged him.

"I love listening to Brooks read. The story is even better in a man's voice," Lalani said when he finished.

"Want me to take the newest chapter?" Argenis asked from the doorway. He, of course, had already heard it. Ciel had shared she always read the newest chapter to her Daddy after finishing one.

"Daddy! You're supposed to be in with the other Daddies. Shoo!" Ciel said, using the papers in her hand to wave him away.

"If I must," Argenis agreed with a smile. "I thought I would offer since I'd come to check on you."

"We're good," Lalani told him, nodding frantically to convince him.

"Perfect." With that, Argenis disappeared back down the hallway.

"Is he gone?" Aurora whispered.

"I've disappeared." Argenis's voice drifted to them from a distance before the front door closed. Brooks had already learned those darn dragons had extremely accurate hearing.

"Okay, here's the latest section. Fingers crossed you like it!" Ciel lifted the paper and shared her newest addition.

Her audience listened in absolute silence as she detailed the main character's illness and her Daddy's treatments. Brooks's focus rose to fix on the ceiling. He couldn't meet anyone's gaze as he struggled to control himself. From the corners of his eyes, he could see the other mates shifting restlessly. Everyone was affected.

When Ciel finished, Skye demanded, "Keep going!"

"I haven't written any more. Sorry, Skye."

"You'll write quickly through, right?" Lalani asked.

Ciel smiled. "As fast as I can. Daddy will only let me work a couple of hours a day. He thinks I need fresh air and sunshine."

"I'm never getting sick," Brooks said softly. The women quickly agreed with that before he added, "I can't believe these books existed, and I never knew. The others can't be as good as Ciel's."

"Thank you, Brooks. There are great stories out there. The ones I found first were on my e-reader," Ciel shared.

"Time to go, Brooks!" Rogan's cheerful voice shattered the hushed atmosphere in the quiet room.

Brooks turned to see him checking out Skye's drawings on the wall. "Um... Do I have to?" He wasn't quite ready to get up yet. His body was hyper alert still.

"Did your feet go to sleep as you laid like that?" Rogan asked. "Let me rescue you."

To Brooks's relief, Rogan stood in front of him to lift Brooks into his arms. His Daddy's bulk shielded the view of his erection from the other mates. Rogan held Brooks tummy-to-tummy in his arms. "Wiggle your feet. That will help."

"I really need to get pillows," Skye mentioned. "Sorry."

"It's okay, Skye. I'll recover soon," Brooks promised before looking back at Rogan to ask, "Are we headed home?"

"Not quite yet. There's a full moon. We thought you all might like to see it," Rogan suggested.

"Nice. I want to check it out," Lalani said, leaping to her feet. "Let me help Ciel, and then I'll be right there."

"Thanks, Ciel," Brooks called as Rogan carried him down

the hallway. Once outside, Rogan walked around the side of the house to set Brooks on his feet.

"Thanks, Daddy."

"I figured you might need some assistance. Take a second, and we'll rejoin the others," Rogan suggested with dancing blue eyes.

"You all knew what we were doing?" Brooks asked.

"Oh, yeah. Argenis clued us in," Rogan said. "She's a good writer?"

"The best. I'd never heard of Daddy books."

"There are some in my library," Rogan told him offhandedly. "Maybe we should read them together."

Brooks could only nod. It was going to take longer now for him to be able to join the others. That idea was even more exciting.

Chapter 15

The dragons had concocted a plan to find May's little brother while the mates had read Ciel's new chapter. Yesterday, a Guardian had reported seeing a small boy she didn't recognize with an older man who seemed to tug him roughly by the hand. She'd followed them around a corner to intervene and lost them.

The Guardian had immediately reported her concerns to those serving as police and peacekeepers. They'd asked the community to keep an eye out for the boy. Three other Wyverns had also alerted the police, concerned by the man's demeanor toward the child. When one attempted to intervene, the older man had threatened her before carrying the child away.

Without power to force water into all areas of the city, manual pumps now supplied the precious commodity in key sections of Wyvern. They had become routine gathering places for the citizens. The authorities had alerted those running the stations to watch out for the youngster. The dragons took it a step further and created a whistled code to alert them.

Days passed with no sightings. Rogan and Brooks visited

Elenore frequently to talk to May and assure her they hadn't forgotten Edwin. She was losing hope and spent hours roaming the streets searching for him.

"I'm going to go to the water stations today, Brooks. Would you like to go with me?" Rogan suggested.

"Yes. I can't imagine what it's been like for May, and for Edwin, of course," Brooks said with a frown.

"We'll continue searching. Someone has to see him soon. The authorities are also working their way throughout Wyvern, asking questions and meeting with people."

"I really want to help. I'll keep my eyes peeled as you fly. Maybe I'll spot something that will assist."

"Good idea." Rogan didn't have the heart to remind him that a dragon's eyesight was greatly superior to a human's. It couldn't hurt for him to scan as well.

On their route to the third water station, Rogan heard the signal. *Hold on!*

As soon as Brooks's arms tightened around his neck, Rogan swerved in that direction. It came from the farthest supply point from Wyvern's old town center. He flew as quickly as he dared without endangering his mate.

Daddy! A truck is hidden under netting back there.

We'll come back and investigate as soon as we check this out, Rogan promised and made a mental note of their approximate location. He landed quickly, and Brooks ran toward those gathered without waiting for him. Shifting, he followed his mate. *Adventurer! Stop! Wait for me!*

His mate didn't slow. Time for another spanking when they were alone.

"That isn't Edwin." Brooks's voice revealed his disappointment as he checked out the blue-eyed boy who'd inspired the alert.

Rogan took a defensive position next to his mate and added,

"Edwin has dark eyes. I'm sorry, ma'am. Could you help us look for a young boy about your son's age with dark hair and eyes? His family is searching for him."

"A lost child? Oh, how sad! Of course, I'll watch for him. His name is Edwin?" she checked.

"Yes, ma'am," Brooks answered. His shoulders drooped with disappointment as the adrenaline seeped from him.

Rogan let the woman drift away with a supply of water before guiding his mate back to a clearing where he could shift. He could see the defeat written on his mate's face.

"I thought we'd found him," Brooks told him softly.

"I did too. False alerts are common, and that's okay. We'd rather those watching for Edwin said something. If they hesitate until they're certain, we could miss him," Rogan reminded him. "Didn't you say you spotted a truck under some kind of cover?"

"Yeah. It was in an alley. Probably just something moved off the street to get it out of the way."

Rogan didn't like the dejection in his mate's voice. "I guess we won't be sure if we don't go check it out. Got anything pressing to fill your schedule for today?"

"No. I was going to help shift some livestock from one field to another. The cows move quickly when they smell dragon on me."

"Of course, they do. Come on, Adventurer. Let's check out what you saw. I made a mental note of roughly where it was so we could find it again," Rogan told him.

A few moments later, Rogan flew over that spot and glimpsed what Brooks had seen. *You're right, Brooks. That's suspicious.* He could make out a white S on a red background.

Without hesitating there, Rogan continued on his trajectory and alerted the horde. *I think Brooks found the Snap-On tools truck. Anyone want to come investigate with me? Keres? Got that fancy suit?*

"Daddy? Aren't we going down there?"

I'm not putting you at risk, Adventurer. I'm going to fly you to the next water station and drop you off. You'll stay there until I come to get you.

"That's totally unfair. I found the truck," Brooks protested as Rogan landed.

You did. Do you want me to locate Edwin or worry about you being hurt or kidnapped?

"I could stay way back away from everything where I could watch but not be in danger," Brooks suggested.

If you're close enough to see, you're close enough to get hit with that powder. I'll keep you updated with messages when I can. Will that be okay?

"Better than nothing," Brooks grumbled before adding, "If I'm far away, I can't help you."

You won't help me like that again, Mate. You are not to put yourself at risk. I will promise to be extremely careful. I don't want to experience that either.

"Promise?"

Promise. I love you, Brooks. Rogan wrapped a wing around Brooks and hugged him close.

"I love you too, Daddy."

Releasing Brooks, Rogan then nudged him toward safety with his snout. Reluctantly, Brooks backed away to give him room to explode into the sky. Rogan could feel his mate's gaze on him until the buildings interrupted their visual connection.

Rogan? Where are you? Keres reached out.

Almost there. I had to safeguard my mate. Look for a truck almost completely covered by netting.

I'm here with Khadar, Argenis messaged. *Check it out for us, Keres.*

In a few minutes, both Keres and Rogan landed a block away from the disguised truck, where the others waited. Keres unrolled a package he'd carried in a leather duffle before dragging out his hazmat suit. Soon, boots, pants, jacket, gloves, and protective hood covered him from head to toe.

The others followed him around the corner. Argenis shifted to flap his wings, driving the wind from them, and prepared to flame any dust that emerged to threaten Keres. The area was quiet. At this time of day, all Wyverns were either embroiled in their chosen line of work to support the community or asleep, preparing for the next night shift.

Keres walked slowly up to the truck. He carefully lifted the edge of the netting and revealed the rest of the tool brand's logo. When he knocked on the side of the truck, something scurried around inside. Thanks to their dragons' keen senses, everyone in the group heard that sound.

Subtle, Keres. Did you want to warn them? Rogan asked.

Only one person moved. Small stature. Keres scanned the truck, searching for any additional traps.

Rogan reconsidered. Maybe Keres wasn't just crazy but crazy smart.

"Edwin? Are you inside?" Keres spoke quietly again. "May sent us."

The scrabbling sound repeated itself but toward Keres this time. Small thumps landed on the metal sides. If the person making that sound was Edwin, he was too young for a complicated discussion. They needed to get him out of there as quickly and as carefully as possible.

"May. May!"

It has to be him. Keres reported. *I'm taking a leap of faith. I think they've abandoned him in this truck to keep him out of sight and booby-trapped it for spite alone. Let's get him out of there.*

Agreement resonating with anger came from each dragon.

Keres moved to the rear of the truck and put out a hand to lift the netting from the back entrance. A smudge of colorful dust made him ease the covering to its original place and step back. *Powder at the rear door.*

Crap! Check the front, Rogan suggested before sending a message to Brooks. *We believe we've found him. Keres is working on the best way to remove him.*

Keres spun and stalked to the front of the truck. Peeking under the netting, he checked the door and turned to shake his head. *They've protected the two entrances to keep us out. Guess what that means, Argenis. You're now officially a welder. Narrow your flame to a tiny beam and let's create our own door in the side. I'll get Edwin to a safer location.*

Keres drew an X on the truck where he wanted Argenis to cut. When the silver dragon nodded, Keres moved a couple of feet toward the front of the truck. Leaning close to the metal side, he said, "Come down here to see May, Edwin. There's going to be some scary stuff happening, but May will keep you safe up here."

Keres tapped on the truck again and waited. A few seconds later, they heard the scrabbling of feet on the metal floor inside the truck. Then a few pats on the wall landed close to Keres.

Go. He's safe.

Argenis sent a laser-fine line of fire toward the truck. Keres knocked on the side again and said, "Stay here with May. She needs you to wait for her with me." A soft thump answered him.

When Argenis has a hole cut, I probably shouldn't lift him out in case I agitated some dust. I'll step away, and Argenis can blast the suit. Khadar, you flap as I take this off. Then, I'll go grab him.

I'll get him. He won't wait while you go through all those steps, Rogan told them.

There's a risk. I did my best not to disturb the dust, Keres warned.

I'll send anything lingering in the opposite direction, Khadar promised. *Keep away from the entrances and keep the wind to your back.*

Almost finished, Argenis alerted them.

Metal rang as the newly crafted door crashed to the floor. A child's face appeared in the opening.

"May?"

Keres held his hand out. "Stay there, Edwin. My buddy, Rogan, is going to come help you down."

Rogan immediately walked toward the truck as Keres stepped to the side to have Argenis torch any lingering dust off the suit. "Hi, Edwin. You have been so brave."

He reached in and carefully lifted the small boy free, avoiding the still glowing edges of the opening. To his relief, Rogan didn't spot any packets of dust attached to Edwin, and the toddler appeared unharmed. Remembering May's pocket of the toxic material, he stripped off the boy's clothing and tossed it to the side for Argenis to destroy.

As he walked toward the others, Rogan removed his shirt and wrapped Edwin in the fabric. "I think he's okay."

"Juice?" Edwin chirped, holding on to Rogan's neck like he'd never let him go.

What should I do with this truck? Argenis asked.

Leave it for now. We'll get some warning signs on it to keep people away. Rogan suggested. *Khadar? Would you fly Edwin and me to Elenore's? I think this young man would like to see his sister. Someone needs to hold him.*

"Juice? May? Bad guys," Edwin said, words tumbling from his mouth in his excitement to be free.

"See what you can get out of him," Keres ordered as he paused in stripping off the suit.

"We'll have time for that later," Rogan suggested. "First, let's get these siblings reunited."

Want me to bring your mate to you? Argenis asked.

Please. Brooks is at the water station about two miles east. Rogan turned to point in the precise direction.

"If you're talking about me, I'm here."

Rogan turned to see a sweaty Brooks stepping out of the shadows from behind them. "You are in so much trouble, Mate." Torn between anger that Brooks had endangered himself and empathy knowing his mate had worried about him, Rogan shook his head.

"I can live with that. I had to make sure you were okay," Brooks said without a shred of an apology in his voice.

What's one more? Come on, the Khadar bus is ready to leave the station, Khadar announced.

When they landed a few moments later, Rogan carried Edwin to the door and knocked.

"Rogan! Brooks! Oh, my. May, come quickly. We have visitors," Elenore called back into the house.

"More people dropping by?" May's unhappy voice drifted down the hallway. When she turned the corner to see Edwin, she shrieked his name and ran forward. Snatching him away from Rogan, she hugged him close, pressing kisses to his cheeks as Edwin patted her face as if he never expected to see her again.

"He's hungry, parched, and dirty, Elenore," Rogan told her.

"I'm used to boys," Brooks's grandmother said with a wink at her grandson. She didn't ask questions but watched the reunion with tears in her eyes. "Food and drink now. Bath later. Questions tomorrow."

"Yes, ma'am." Rogan wouldn't argue with her. "Is it okay if they stay with you?"

May pivoted to listen to Elenore's answer. Her guarded expression hinted at how precarious their life had been in the past.

"You're going to have to use dynamite to get them out of this house. May and Edwin are home now," Elenore said firmly and wrapped her arm around May's waist. "Come on. We have cookies to eat."

"Juice?" Edwin asked hopefully.

"I have just what a thirsty boy wants," Elenore assured him as she steered the group to the kitchen.

Rogan watched the chattering trio leave the hallway. They looked good together. Elenore would enjoy the youngsters as much as they needed her stability and willingness to share her home. A weight lifted from his shoulders that Edwin and May were reunited again.

Chapter 16

Of course, Keres had put that hazmat suit back on after they left and checked out the truck. He'd reported nothing remained inside except for a few open bottles of water and an empty box of animal crackers. The entire horde fumed. And, if they were smart, the scum who had left a little boy in a sealed truck should never show up near his adoptive grandma.

Brooks sat in a swing in Rogan's backyard and tried to figure out why a group would hate the dragons so much. They protected Wyvern. Who would want to kill them? The answer was obvious—only those who were prevented from doing what they wanted by the dragons would work to eliminate them.

"Don't forget the fanatics and the anti-dragon crew," Rogan reminded him. "There are those who believe we are aberration against nature for shifting from human to beast forms."

"I hate it when you eavesdrop on my thoughts," Brooks said, frowning at the shifter, who lounged nearby against the tree trunk.

"We were both focused on the same subject. Your mind screamed at me. I couldn't tune it out."

"Do you think we're going to find them?" Brooks asked.

"They'll screw up badly at some point. They didn't plan on dragons' hoarding powers. That hazmat outfit of Keres's came in handy. It could be at the end of its life now. Being blasted by dragon fire twice is way past its intended usage. Keres survived, but a human would have roasted inside that suit."

"Are you all searching for another one?"

"Yes. Someone will find some in a firehouse or a warehouse. Speaking of supplies... Would you like to go search for a pharmacy that has your grandmother's meds?" Rogan asked.

"You'll take me with you?"

"Definitely. You can hold the list of what the doctors have requested," Rogan suggested. "Do you need anything? More jeans? Some T-shirts? Your traveling lifestyle with only what you could carry didn't allow you to have many extras. I have some...."

"I don't really need anything," Brooks interrupted him. "They have that clothing exchange set up in town. I could grab something there. Others may benefit from items more than I do."

"Okay. Let's go. Want to run inside first?"

"Yes!" Brooks jumped out of the swing on its next forward motion and raced for the house. Rogan followed at a slower pace. He had a few necessities on his list to get for his mate but now thought of an addition.

In a few minutes, Rogan flew through the clouds. While the attacks from the border had decreased, there were still a few determined militants who attempted to injure the dragons as they left Wyvern. Rogan didn't rise to the altitude he normally chose in order to protect his mate from the cold.

Heading toward the west, Rogan searched for an abandoned town. He didn't want to take supplies from humans who gathered there. It didn't take long to find a suburb with no activity.

Rogan

When I land, don't slide off immediately. Keep an eye in each direction. Let's make sure it's safe.

When no one came out to greet or attack them, Rogan glanced back at Brooks. *Okay. Stand next to me. I'll shift quickly.*

Taking care not to injure his mate, Rogan switched forms. "Stay behind me and be ready to find shelter."

"Rogan? Should we leave?"

"We need medicine, remember? This looks harmless, but if it isn't, don't do anything heroic. Find a protected place to shelter and let me deal with the attackers."

"Do you remember I traveled all over the world before we met?"

"I do, Adventurer. Unfortunately, people are more desperate now," Rogan reminded him.

Brooks opened his mouth to argue only to snap it closed. He couldn't debate that truth.

Rogan led the way through the smashed glass entry doors. Businesses had faced a choice in the days after the change. Either leave the doors open for visitors to help themselves or be ransacked. Some had held on, hoping technology would come back online and everything would be as it had existed before. Others had simply taken what their family needed and walked away. This was obviously an owner who'd delayed sharing the provisions with those who'd needed it. From the large rusty brown stain on the floor, safeguarding this store had been fatal. Rogan shifted to block Brooks's view.

"The first looters searched for narcotics. Antibiotics and things like blood pressure meds weren't in big demand. If we're lucky, no one has returned for that now urgent need," Rogan told him.

The metal barriers protecting the pharmacy gaped open from massive blows of what Rogan guessed was an axe. He pulled apart the edges to make it easier to slide between before stepping inside. Reaching a hand back, he guided Brooks through safely as well.

"Okay. Pharmacists usually store drugs by how they're administered—tablets in one area, injectables in another, etc. Let's begin with tablets."

He snagged a plastic bag from the dispenser and handed Brooks a list. "Start checking alphabetically for these."

A few minutes later, Brooks announced, "I have the first item on the list. There are two large bottles. One unopened, the other half-full."

"Leave the open one for someone else. Grab the other container. If there's only a single jar, take it," Rogan decided.

Soon, Brooks held a bulging bag. "I found all the medicine except one of the generics we wanted."

"Perfect." Rogan had several tote bags stuffed with other supplies the doctors had requested. "We have a few over-the-counter items to locate on the shelf, and we'll get out of here." It was no surprise that the first thing he checked for was additional allergy medicine for Brooks.

As they walked through the aisles, Brooks announced, "No diapers and formula."

"Those probably went fast."

"Toilet paper is gone too." Brooks pointed to the candy selection. "Those disgusting circus peanuts are still on the shelf. No one likes those. Everything chocolate has disappeared."

His mate's voice sounded so sad that Rogan stopped in the grocery section and snagged a tub of cocoa powder. His cook could make a chocolatey treat for Brooks. One last stop in the personal aisle and Rogan grabbed the last three tubes of lubricant.

"Let's take these for the girls," Brooks suggested, pointing to two last boxes of tampons on the shelf.

"I've got a case at home. We'll leave these for someone without supplies," Rogan told him.

"Why do you have a case?"

"Dragons collect useful things. My mate could have been female."

Brooks was quiet as they walked back to the front of the store. Rogan suspected his mate was worried about something. "Is there anything else you need or want?"

A sound caught his attention. He pulled Brooks behind him as he zeroed in on that noise. Two people.

"We've left lots of supplies. There's plenty for both of us," Rogan called.

"Now, that doesn't work for us. We want it all." A man's voice answered, and he laughed. "We're armed and not afraid to shoot you. Drop what you have and walk out. We might let you leave without extra holes in your body."

"I'm afraid those options don't work for us. Here's your choice. Put down your weapons and clear out or I'll let my dragon flambe you." Rogan offered his options in a pleasant tone.

"Right. Because so many dragons are pets. Does he like belly rubs too?" a higher-pitched female voice asked sarcastically.

"He does. Those scales get itchy," Rogan said, gesturing for Brooks to get down lower. His mate followed his instructions for once without argument before plucking a can of bath salts from the bottom shelf.

Jerking to the side, Rogan avoided a gunshot as he changed into his dragon form. Instantly, he allowed his dragon to take over. Knocking shelving over like dominoes and ripping out ceiling tiles, the red dragon created his own space in the large drugstore. A loud, pain-filled shout echoed inside the store. Rogan swiveled his head. One of the two hadn't moved fast enough from between the aisles.

"Help! I can't breathe," their assailant wheezed.

Rogan focused on the other guy. Rage brewed inside him. One of them had fired at his mate, putting his life in danger. Rogan stalked forward, causing havoc with each giant foot he set down with a ground-jarring thump. Smoke leaked through his nostrils.

Flaming the last attacker would set the interior of the store on fire, destroying all its contents, including the items Wyvern needed. Rogan could escape through the ceiling with his mate, if necessary. He wouldn't be able to rescue the drugs and supplies they'd collected. He'd try intimidation first.

As he moved toward the hidden foe, a second gunshot sounded. It slammed into his side and ricocheted off his scales, not injuring Rogan in the least but pissing him off completely. As he turned to eliminate the man pinned under the shelving unit, a projectile whizzed past his snout to smack into the attacker's forehead with a solid thump. A second thud followed as the man's head struck the floor. He didn't move this time. Scurrying footsteps sounded as the other ran for the door.

Good shot, Adventurer.

"I was the star pitcher of the Wyvern baseball team in high school," Brooks told him, feeling ten feet tall for having eliminated a bad guy.

Of course you were. Let's get back to Wyvern, shall we?

"Yes, Daddy."

Chapter 17

Brooks sang on the way home—not because he was celebrating surviving the attack but because he wanted to keep Rogan from reading his thoughts. When he spotted the walls surrounding Wyvern, he asked, *Can you drop me off at home, Daddy, before you turn over the supplies to the doctors?*

Don't you want to go see your grandmother?

Not today. I'm tired. I think I'll take a nap, Brooks told him, yawning widely.

Do you feel okay? Weird vibes are coming my way.

I'm fine. I didn't sleep well last night.

Rogan was quiet for a few seconds before he asked, *Are you worried about something, Brooks?*

No. I'm just tired, Daddy.

You can talk to me about anything, Brooks.

I know.

Okay. I'll come in and tuck you in before I go.

No need. I don't want to delay you. I'll crawl into bed, Brooks insisted as Rogan landed. Brooks quickly slid down to the ground and turned to go inside.

Would you take Daddy's things and put them in the nurs-

ery? Rogan asked, lifting his right front claws that held several bags.

Of course. Brooks quickly checked for the bag containing the cocoa and the tubes of lubricant. He discovered Rogan had slipped a bottle of bubble gum scented bubble bath into the bag. That seemed like a perfect gift for a female mate. Brooks forced himself to smile and waved the bag.

"Got it! See you in a while."

He walked slowly to the front door, yawning twice when Rogan's gaze met his. Once inside, he dropped off the cocoa with the cook and left everything else in the nursery. Grabbing his dragon, Rogue, Brooks headed for a different floor and let himself into a guest room. He could hide in here for a while.

Taking a seat on the closet floor in the dark, Brooks retraced his steps to that door in his brain. He reached for the second latch and resealed it. It didn't click completely closed, but the connection between them narrowed. Hopefully, Rogan couldn't read his thoughts and emotions now. That seemed way too intimate for someone who would have rather been with a female mate. Hopefully, it wouldn't alert Rogan that something was wrong. He should think Brooks was asleep.

Dropping his head down on his knees, Brooks felt like his heart was breaking. He was torn in two different directions—loving his mate while thinking he wasn't right for him. Brooks hugged his stuffie close and tried to pull himself together. Rogan would return soon. He might give him a bit of alone time to wake up from his nap, but they usually spent the evening together. Could Brooks keep the charade going that nothing was wrong and that he felt Rogan cared for him as much as he would have cherished a female mate?

Rogan had shared with him he had a male mate before him. Brooks hadn't thought of asking if he was disappointed to have another one. Rogan had always seemed attracted to him, but now, Brooks replayed their conversations in his mind. He'd told Brooks he loved him very quickly. Had he lied? Was Rogan pretending to care about him?

Little things seemed big as Brooks reflected on them.

A crashing noise came from the front of the house, making Brooks sit up straight.

Brooks! Where are you? Rogan's urgent call filled Brooks's conscious.

Brooks fought to clear his head. He imagined the color gray, hoping it would cover anything floating around in his mind. Aware he couldn't hide forever, Brooks stood. As soon as he got his thoughts protected, he'd call Rogan like he'd woken up a few minutes ago.

"Brooks! Answer me!"

Rogan sounded upset. Had there been another attack? Maybe one of the mates was hurt. Brooks pulled himself together and headed for the staircase. He'd gotten halfway down the hall when Rogan appeared in front of him.

"Brooks! Our bond dwindled to almost nothing. I thought someone had shielded you." Rogan hugged him hard, knocking the breath from Brooks's lungs. He stepped back while holding on to Brooks's arms like he was afraid he'd disappear.

"Maybe it blinked out while I was asleep," Brooks suggested and yawned for special effect.

"Tell me what's going on. You've closed off our connection as much as you could. Only a deliberate act would cause this."

"Perhaps we don't have as strong a relationship as you did with your other mates. I'm sure it happens. You have to get tired of being stuck with someone. Fate might not always be right."

"What are you talking about, Adventurer?" Rogan shook Brooks gently. "What is going on in your mind?"

Brooks met his gaze for the first time. "It's okay, Rogan. I understand."

"What the fuck do you understand? Because I don't!"

Brooks leaned back slightly from the volume of that exasperated question. Why was he so upset?

"Sir, can I help you?" Sara's gentle voice asked from the stairway.

"No!" Rogan shouted and then shook his head as he visibly tried to pull himself together. "I'm sorry, Sara. There's something wrong, and I need to get to the bottom of it. I won't hurt Brooks. Just give us some privacy."

"Of course you won't, sir. Mates are the most precious of your treasures."

"If I were a woman," Brooks grumbled.

"What?" Rogan's roar cleared the hallway as Sara hurried away. "What does your masculinity have to do with how much I love you?"

Brooks shrugged, hoping to knock Rogan's hold off. Rogan's fingers tightened around him. "It's okay, Rogan. I understand everyone has preferences. I'm sorry you got stuck with me."

"I am not fucking stuck with you! I would not change a single thing about you."

"Right," Brooks said. "You kind of have to say that."

"I do not!" Rogan glared at him. "What put this in your mind? You were fine before we went to the drugstore. Did you take something there? Do you have a drug problem? I can help with that."

"What? No! I'm not an addict."

"Then what happened? One moment we're discussing circus peanuts, then we're attacked. Wait... Did something happen when they shot at us?" Rogan leaned forward to sniff him. "I don't smell blood. Are you hurt?"

"No, Rogan. I'm not physically injured."

Rogan

"So, there's mental damage?" Rogan asked softly. His voice shifted immediately, warm and caring. "Talk to me. Let me help."

"Rogan! I'm not mentally *damaged*." Brooks stressed that last word before continuing, "Other than being hit over the head with the fact you wish your mate was a woman."

Rogan shook his head. "That's completely untrue. Where did you get that idea?"

"Come on, Rogan. Who stockpiles tampons? You were obviously planning for a female mate and got stuck with me."

"Will you come with me? There's something I should have shared with you," Rogan said quietly.

"Will it make a difference?" Brooks asked skeptically.

"I hope so."

"Okay." Brooks agreed with another shrug.

Rogan took his hand and tugged him to the stairs. Brooks followed him to the main floor and then toward the back entrance of the mansion. The shifter turned into a small closet-like room only to stop at a piece of art created from thousands of small pieces of stone meticulously placed together. Rogan glided his fingers over the fragments, pressing here and there in a seemingly random pattern.

When Rogan pressed on the mosaic, the entire wall grumbled before swinging open. Rogan walked forward into the darkness, drawing Brooks along with him. Once the wall closed behind him, Rogan exhaled a stream of fire to ignite a torch.

"Come, Adventurer. I considered sharing this with you earlier, but I wanted to make sure it was prepared for you. This staircase will take us under the mansion. After your reaction to the dust in my hoard, Sara and my staff have scrubbed this area from ceiling to floor. It is now safe for you."

"Rogan, I don't see how the basement is going to help."

"I know you don't. Do this for me, please."

"Okay. You don't have to explain, Rogan. It's okay. I understand that all mates aren't perfect."

"You don't understand anything if you believe that." Rogan corrected him sharply before softening his tone. "Come with me, Adventurer."

"Fine. Lead on."

The stairs wound farther and farther down until Brooks wondered how deep underground they'd go. Finally, the stairs ended, and darkness stretched before them. Rogan urged him forward, leading the way. As they walked through the shadowy tunnel, Rogan lit the torches spaced along the way.

A dark opening appeared ahead in the tunnel to the left. Rogan ducked inside and lit the torch inside. A picture hung on the wall. It was a good-looking man dressed in old-fashioned clothing. Drawn forward by curiosity, Brooks stepped closer.

The man wasn't classically handsome. His appearance wouldn't have made anyone check him out. Big and brawny, his occupation must have required great strength.

"That's Ian. I've told you about him. He was my first mate from Wyvern. When fate matched us together, the founding fathers tried to pull out of the deal. They hadn't anticipated one of their sons would be a mate." Rogan's voice sounded soft and gentle as he gazed at the portrait on the wall.

"You loved him," Brooks guessed.

"I have loved all my mates."

"There was something special about him."

"Mates are always unique. Dragons live eons and have several mates. We never forget our time with each one."

"But Ian stands out because he was your first Wyvern?" Brooks kept pushing. A different vibe flowed from Rogan that told him this was important.

"Ian was my first fated mate. I was young and cocky. Not a virgin—far from it. Ian did not wish to be a mate. It was extremely difficult for a male to admit he was attracted to a male in those days—even with the special circumstance of a mating bond. Of course, no one understood the bond then either."

"He wasn't gay."

"No. He was quite popular with the ladies. As the apprentice of Wyvern's blacksmith, Ian took care of putting on horseshoes. Business flourished with him in the shop," Rogan said with a smile.

"And when the mate bond snapped into place?"

"The blacksmith had to train someone new. Ian didn't adjust well to a life of leisure. The town treated him differently, of course—polite and still thankful for supporting Wyverns as a mate, but his new lifestyle wasn't understood."

Brooks could read the grief on Rogan's face. "What happened to Ian?"

"He died happily at 154. I still miss him after all these years. I think because of the hardship that characterized our first days, we learned to depend on each other exclusively. We were more than close."

A heavy quiet filled the room as they both considered Rogan's words. After several long seconds, Rogan said, "Let's continue."

Rogan led Brooks through each of the small chambers dedicated to his mates. In each one, he shared some information about his mate. Brooks could tell that he honestly loved each individual and had treasured their time together.

"Is it rare to have a male mate since you've had more female ones?" Brooks asked after the last chamber.

"Rare? I've never crunched the numbers. It's possible that the pool of females in Wyvern is larger to draw from. Or maybe other dragons have male mates while I have a female, so the total balances?"

"Or you haven't allowed yourself to have another male mate," Brooks suggested, pulling that idea out of the air.

Rogan looked at him in shock. Ten seconds of heavy silence later, he nodded. "Yes. That's what I believed. Until now."

"You mean me?" Brooks asked, completely taken by surprise.

"Yes. We are fated mates because I needed you. Perhaps more than I've ever needed a mate."

"Because I'm a guy?"

"Because you are the total package—intuitive, adventurous, fearless, sexy, and curious. I needed someone to make me see the world differently. Someone who would challenge me. Ian did that in his way."

"I'm a replacement for him?" Brooks asked, shaking his head.

"Absolutely not. Ian was what I required in that day. He wouldn't be now. Just like you wouldn't have been right in his time."

Brooks relaxed. That made sense. "So now, this is what you want? A woman wouldn't be better?"

"Have you met any woman like you, Adventurer?"

After allowing an audible puff of air to escape his lips to express his doubt, Brooks admitted, "Probably not. I've always strayed away from the paths most people find comfortable."

"Exactly. Obviously, fate knew that you are who I needed in my life now." Rogan stepped forward and drew Brooks close. "When you closed that second lock, I couldn't feel you. Dragons don't get scared, but that shook me."

"I'm sorry." Brooks wanted to kick himself for causing Rogan pain but forced himself to ask again. "Are you sure you wouldn't choose to be with a female mate?"

"I want to be with you, Adventurer. You are everything I need and so much more to enjoy. Think carefully. Have I given you a hint that I wished you were something other than yourself?" Rogan's gaze blazed into his.

"You stockpiled tampons," he blurted.

"Yes. I have collected many items to care for my mate. Dragons hoard more than money, jewels, and swords. Come. Let me show you," Rogan said, moving to Brooks's side as he wrapped his arm around his back.

Rogan guided him to an arched doorway where an ancient wooden door guarded whatever was on the other side. His mate pressed a stone into the wall and uncovered a thick skeleton key. Unlocking the door, he pushed it open and ushered Brooks inside.

"It was much more impressive when the florescent lights worked," Rogan mentioned before walking inside to roam around lighting torches. "Grab a basket and fill it up."

After watching the torches illuminate the ceiling that seemed to extend forever, Brooks stepped into the aisles. He scanned all the things loaded onto the shelves. Facial tissue, toilet paper, makeup, athlete's foot cream, slightly underinflated footballs and soccer balls, golf clubs, sunscreen, gummy candy.... Brooks couldn't spot the end of the supplies gathered in this area. The rows kept going and going.

Rogan reappeared at his side and peered into the basket Brooks carried. "You didn't find anything you wanted?"

"This is overwhelming, Rogan. How did you get all this down here?"

"There's a door where trucks used to pull up with deliveries."

"Does it fill the entire mountain?"

"Of course not. It's only this level," Rogan assured him.

"Only on *this* level," Brooks repeated as he leaned to the side to see if he could spot the end of the row. He could not.

"There's so much here. Why'd you pick up lubricant and bubble bath?"

"Habit, I guess. Collecting is what I do."

"Do you have any guy stuff stockpiled?" Brooks asked suspiciously.

"I have a bunch of action video games and systems. Those don't work anymore. I do have a section of those building blocks that snap together to make famous buildings. Is that a guy thing?"

"You have LEGOs?" Brooks asked in amazement.

"Yes. Those still work, don't they? Some of those sets have so many pieces. It would be fun to put those together as a team. Want to go check them out?"

"Please." Brooks had loved LEGOs since he was a kid. His on-the-go lifestyle wasn't convenient to carry the enormous sets around with him. Becoming a mate allowed him to travel with Rogan and return to Wyvern as his home base.

When Rogan stopped in front of a massive display of toys, Brooks couldn't believe it. He felt like he'd won the lottery. "You have so many fun things here."

"Yes. I hope so. Taking care of my mate is vital. If you can't locate a set here, we'll put it on a list and go exploring to find it," Rogan assured him.

"So, the tampons weren't because you were focused on having a female mate?" Brooks double-checked.

"No more than the hemorrhoid cream reflects my need to have a mate that doesn't eat enough fiber," Rogan joked.

"I really messed up, didn't I?"

"Only if we hadn't worked together to fix this. If something bothers you, talk to me, Brooks."

"I will, Daddy," he promised. He felt silly and so sorry he'd gotten confused—and appreciative that his Daddy had forced him to talk and figure this out. Brooks could have ruined everything.

"I love to hear you use that name for me. Let's sit down and open those locks again. My heart hurts from being separated from you," Rogan shared.

"Mine too."

Rogan settled on the ground and drew Brooks onto his lap. He held him close as Brooks retraced his steps to that door. This time, Brooks tore the second lock off. He never wanted to separate them again.

Chapter 18

"Could we have the mates over here?" Brooks asked a few weeks later as he and Rogan ate breakfast together. Without any attacks or strange things happening, the dragons hadn't had a reason to gather. That was good, but Brooks was getting bored staying home.

"Would you like to meet everyone for pizza?"

"I haven't had pizza in forever." Brooks sighed. A thought popped into his mind, and he sat up straight. "I wonder if Angelino's is open."

"It is. We've met there before. Want me to organize a meal there?"

"Yes. Can we go today?"

"I'll contact Angelino to see if he can squeeze us in. He might need supplies," Rogan cautioned.

"Let's go talk to him," Brooks suggested.

"We've got a few hours until he's at the restaurant. Let me check with the others and see what's possible. Finish your breakfast, Brooks."

"I'd rather fill up on pizza at lunch."

"Finish your cereal, Brooks. You don't want your bottom to be as red as the tomato sauce on that pizza."

Brooks shook his head empathically. He definitely didn't want that. Jumping to do what his Daddy requested, he picked up his spoon. "Yes, Daddy." Brooks quickly finished his cornflakes and lifted the bowl to drain the milk. "Are we going to go visit the others to check with them?"

"I've already sent a message to the horde. We'll hear back soon."

"Okay. Can I go play outside?" Brooks asked.

Rogan hesitated, and Brooks guessed what he was thinking about. After attackers had taken Skye from the lawn of Oldrik and Ardon's mountain, Rogan made sure that either himself or an armed member of his staff supervised his activities. Rogan tried to be subtle about guarding him, but they both knew.

"I want to run down to the barn. Loads of people are milling in that area. I've heard newborn kittens are there."

"No kittens in the house. One will run by my face in the middle of the night, and that will be the end of the fuzzy butt," Rogan decreed.

"What? You'd snap and chomp on him?"

"I might."

"You would not. You don't forget I'm sleeping with you and eat me," Brooks corrected him.

"Sure I do. And we both enjoy it," Rogan teased.

Brooks glanced around to see if anyone listened to their conversation. Thankfully, they were alone. He whispered, "We do love it," before adding, "Come on, Rogan. I'll be fine."

"Send me a message when you get there, and when you're returning," Rogan directed.

With a cheeky salute, Brooks agreed, "Yes, sir!" He jumped up and ran out before Rogan could reconsider.

The fresh air and sunshine felt good on his skin. Brooks jogged to the barn, calling greetings to each person he met along the way. At the door, he remembered to contact Rogan. *I'm here. All is well.*

Thank you, Adventurer.

He turned in a slow circle, searching for the kittens. The momma cat strolled out from between two hay bales to wrap around his legs. "Hi. May I visit your kittens?" he asked as he leaned over to pet her silky fur.

A few seconds later, a small face peeked out at him. Brooks sat down on the floor and held out his hand, but the kitten disappeared. The momma cat sprawled out next to him and rolled, silently asking for belly rubs. Of course, he lavished them on her as he kept an eye out for the kittens.

Brooks could hear them scurrying behind the hay bales. Scanning the stacks, he saw an orange face peering at him from around a corner. There must be a couple of entrances. With another pat to the mama cat, he stood and walked around the stack. In a niche missing several bales, the kittens played.

Grinning, he enjoyed their antics for a few minutes to make sure he'd counted all of them. Fluffy and different colors, the small creatures enchanted Brooks. He'd never had a pet as a child. Later when he traveled around, it hadn't seemed fair to a dog to drag it from one place to another. Now, it appeared that he was staying here for a while. Maybe....

Settling on the ground once again, Brooks held out a hand, wiggling his fingers to attract the kittens. The orange kitten pounced on him immediately. The others came forward more slowly after they'd decided he was safe. By that time, Marmalade already had a name and had curled up on Brooks's lap to snooze.

I think I have a cat now, Brooks sent to Rogan. The image

of dragon jaws snapping the kitten projected to him in return made Brooks laugh. Rogan wouldn't munch on Marmalade.

He wondered when the kittens would be old enough to be separated from their mother. Someone had to know more than he did. He'd ask a few people working on the estate. Brooks scooped up the friendly kitten and placed him in the pile of now dozing siblings. He'd come back to visit each day to make sure Marmalade didn't forget him.

Glancing up, he saw something black on top of one of the bales stacked near the ceiling. That wasn't a kitten, was it? Concerned that it had gotten stranded up there, Brooks chose a good path and started climbing. When he reached the top, he figured out it was a black piece of cloth. Brooks sat down on a bale as he untangled the black material from the twine. He'd save someone else from making the climb to rescue a kitten.

From his perch at the top of the barn, Brooks could see both entrances. A man walked in and circled around the bales searching. The man's posture and body language, even from above, alerted him that something was wrong. He shifted as quietly as possible to lie down out of sight.

"Did you see him come out?" a strident voice asked.

"I didn't, but he's not in here. He must have snuck out when you were distracted," a second voice accused.

"Hey, I had to talk to the foreman when he approached. It's not like I can tell him I'm too busy watching the dragon's mate to hear what you have to say."

"Whatever. We're alone. What's the update to the plan?"

"A supply of powder is coming in tomorrow as part of a shipment of gardening equipment. The guards are getting lax about checking the crates, so it's probable that they won't detect it. And if they do, they'll die."

Immediately when he heard the word powder, Brooks

Rogan

messaged Rogan, sending a small burst of information when the man naturally paused, so he could continue listening. *Barn. Two guys. Powder.*

Brooks ignored Rogan's burst of anger and concern to pay attention to the conversation.

"Then what? Did they figure out how to get rid of all the dragons at once?"

"Yeah. It's brilliant."

"You're not going to tell me?"

Brooks peeked over the edge. The two men stood almost directly below him, wearing hats. He couldn't see their faces. Damn. Without recognizing their voices, he wouldn't be able to pick them out of a crowd. Crossing his fingers, he hoped Rogan would arrive soon. Movement at the door caught his attention, and Brooks descended stealthily from the bales.

"What's going on here?" Rogan demanded.

"Sorry, sir. We were coordinating our jobs. We'll get back to work now." The spokesman and his collaborator turned to leave through the other door.

Brooks dropped to the ground in front of the other doorway to block it. "I don't think so." Without taking his eyes off the men, he called to the dragon shifter, "Rogan, there's a plan to smuggle in powder in a shipment of shovels and stuff."

"Your mate must have misunderstood. We were discussing grabbing the rakes to blend in the fertilizer for the next crops," the same man said casually, like it was no big deal.

Brooks couldn't prove what he'd heard. He crossed his fingers, hoping his Daddy would believe him. *I know what they said, Rogan. I'm not imagining this.*

"How are you getting messages from outside Wyvern?" Rogan asked, strolling forward to keep the men in sight. "Where's the powder coming from?"

"Nowadays, there's no way to communicate with anyone outside Wyvern, sir. And powder? What's that?"

"They definitely weren't discussing fertilizer," Brooks pointed out.

"Sorry, sirs. We're confused and don't know what you're talking about. If you'll excuse us." The second man tried to edge around Brooks, obviously deeming him less dangerous.

Brooks braced an arm on the doorframe, blocking him. "I don't think we're done with you."

The man moved so fast. In a split second, he had a knife at Brooks's throat as he held him pinned against his chest. "I *think* you're done with me. I'm going to walk out of here."

"It's a long distance to the border," Rogan said softly. He sounded calm, but his eyes glowed red.

"I'll take a horse and your mate to make sure you don't get any ideas." The other man sidled behind Brooks's attacker to shield himself.

"You're right that I won't do anything to endanger my mate. You've forgotten that threatening or putting a dragon's mate in peril is an act punishable by death," Rogan pointed out.

"I can slit his throat before you can get to me. Then we both die."

"Hey, let's avoid anyone dying," Brooks suggested. He tried to sound amused, but his voice was stressed, even to his own ears.

The knife blade pressed harder to his throat, and a prickle of pain stung his skin. "Shut up, mate," his attacker spat out. The man made that word sound like a four-letter curse.

The ground shuddered below their feet in three waves. Brooks recognized the sensation. Dragons had landed. The tremor rattled the two men. The one holding Brooks glanced around wildly.

Drop, Brooks. Now!

Rogan

Brooks hesitated. A thin line of fire blazed past Brooks's head. So close, Brooks could hear and smell his hair sizzle. His attacker screamed and shook. When the arm holding him relaxed, Brooks pushed the knife from his throat and dropped to the ground. A second later, he heard a thump, and the man's knee hit his back. Brooks glanced over his shoulder to see a crumpled body lying behind him. The knife stained with his blood had dropped into the scattering of hay on the floor.

Brooks! Come here!

This time, he moved immediately. As he scrambled to distance himself, a hand grabbed at his biceps, but Brooks wrenched his arm away, hitting the ground. His fingers brushed the fallen knife. Automatically, his fingers closed around the handle, and he pulled the blade up to defend himself as he pivoted to face the second man.

No way! He wasn't going to be a hostage ever again.

"Get away from me," Brooks growled.

Just me, Mate, Rogan reassured him as his arm wrapped around Brooks to toss him several feet behind him into the hay.

The man shrank from the dragon shifter, innately sensing that running from the beast would be the last thing he did. "I can tell you what they're planning. Kill me and you'll be clueless until it happens."

"Rogan, let us take him away, and you can see to your mate." Drake's voice sounded from behind them. Rogan didn't take his gaze from his prey.

"He attacked Brooks," Rogan snarled.

"He will pay for that," Keres assured him, appearing behind the culprit.

"Wait! No! I'm not going to tell you anything if you hurt me," the man yelled.

"You're going to share every detail," Oldrik promised. "The

amount of pain required to get the truth is completely up to you."

"Keres? Will you take care of tying this guy up so he can't do anything stupid?" Drake asked, pulling a length of rope from the wall and tossing it to Keres.

"On it."

"Hey! Watch it. Oof! That's too tight! You're going to cut off my blood supply."

"You don't need those hands to talk," Keres pointed out and continued binding the man into a neat, tidy package that a dragon could easily transport.

The pounding of Brooks's heart slowed, and he could feel his blood pressure coming down as the shock and adrenaline ebbed. A purring visitor had come to check on him as soon as he'd landed. Instinctively soothing Brooks, Marmalade busily rubbed against his face and licked his hair. Curling his fingers in the silky fur, Brooks told himself it was over. He needed one more thing.

Daddy?

Rogan whirled at that messaged plea and raced to his mate's side. Brooks sat on the bale of hay where Rogan had tossed him, but now an orange tabby kitten curled up in his lap. "Are you okay, Adventurer?"

"I think I'm done with adventures for a long time, Daddy," Brooks whispered. "I'm fine."

"Let me see where he cut you," Rogan demanded, gently tilting Brooks's chin up. His fingers smoothed softly over the stinging injury. "You're all right, Mate. Let's get this cleaned up so it doesn't get infected."

"Can Marmalade come?" Brooks wasn't quite ready to let the purring kitten go.

"Marmalade, huh?"

"I'm guessing you have a cat now, Rogan. He's already got a name," Drake observed.

Rogan rolled his eyes at that observation. "I knew I had a cat the minute Brooks came here to visit them," Rogan answered, acknowledging the creature's place in his household. "Marmalade can come to the house for a visit while we get you doctored up. Then his mama will want him back."

"Okay," Brooks agreed. As long as he didn't have to give the sweet kitten up yet, it would be okay. "Can I sleep here with him?"

"No, Brooks. You will each snooze in your own beds for a couple more weeks. Come on. Let's show Marmalade the house. Maybe he'll decide he'd rather stay in the barn," Rogan suggested as he helped Brooks to his feet.

The kitten meowed his denial of that suggestion, as if he understood what they were discussing. Brooks couldn't imagine how the small creature could get cuter. He loved Marmalade already.

"I'll haul this guy to my mountain for questioning," Keres stated.

"I'll take him," Drake declared.

"Fine. You have all the fun. I've got other things to do. Call if you need help," Keres offered.

"I'll keep that in mind," Drake told him as Rogan led Brooks from the barn.

Brooks didn't look back. The dragons would take care of the bad guy. He bumped his shoulder into his Daddy's as they walked.

"Thanks for believing me."

Immediately, Rogan wrapped an arm around his waist and said, "Of course, Adventurer. I love you."

"I love you too. Life is pretty exciting as a mate," Brooks commented.

"I hope this threat will be eliminated soon, Mate. I need you to be safe. I'm too old for this excitement."

"I've meant to talk to you about your gray scales."

"What gray scales?" Rogan thundered.

"Just kidding, Daddy." Brooks checked in on the kitten in his arms after all that noise. Marmalade didn't react. He'd fit their lives perfectly.

Epilogue

Keres shifted and waited for Oldrik to arrive. He'd put off this moment for as long as possible. Now with black thoughts pummeling him from all sides, Keres needed to act now. The bronze dragon's wings reflected the sunlight as he landed.

"Oldrik. Thank you for meeting me."

"I don't enjoy disguising anything from my mate and Ardon. You said this was urgent," the dragon shifter flatly stated.

"Tell me where your sister is." Keres got straight to the point.

"Why?" Oldrik asked bluntly.

"You know why. It's the end for me. I'll replace myself for the horde."

"Your mate might be on the next transport," Oldrik pointed out.

"The numbers of those coming back to Wyvern have dwindled to a handful every month. The list of missing Wyverns is blank, except for a few older people. There are no arriving mates now, Oldrik. I have to face the truth. There isn't a mate for me in this generation. I can't last for another one. It's over for me. Tell me where she is."

"I can't do that for her safety, Keres."

"I will swear an oath to you. Over many years, I've proven to you my word, once given, is solid. That hasn't changed. I will treat her well."

"I'm not even sure where she is."

"Whatever you can share will help. I'll find her," Keres assured him. "I just need a hint of where to start."

Keres studied Oldrik's expression as the bronze dragon considered his options. Rare female dragons battled for survival as shifters doomed to madness sought them as a last option. He couldn't imagine a life that didn't involve flight and freedom—all those things that a dragon craved. For eons, females existed only to bring new dragons into the world. The procreation process couldn't be easy for them, taken by a dragon barely holding on to sanity without a mate bond to make it pleasurable.

Keres met Oldrik's gaze. "I will plead my case with your sister and hope she will help. I will accept no as an answer. Death will come to me either way. I will not drag an innocent into the torture that besieges me."

"I have your word on that?" Oldrik's focus was laser sharp.

"You have my oath."

"The last I heard, she was in a small hilltop in Montana. Rimi mentioned the construction of a new sports arena that might force her to move."

"Thank you, Oldrik."

"Bring her back, Keres. She deserves to live in the light."

Keres met his gaze and nodded. There wouldn't be a good end for him, but perhaps something positive could come out of this. The horde would protect his offspring and Oldrik's sister.

Rogan

After the threat to his mate, Rogan isolated Brooks from others as he investigated whether more on his staff were involved with the two men who'd plotted against them. No one else had joined his employment during that same time period. Those two had come seeking work with a sad story of needing to feed their families. His supervisor wouldn't fall for that in the future. Rogan would insist on serious investigations into any applicant's past.

Twenty-four-hour patrols of the border resumed. Their enemies still plotted to bring danger into Wyvern. The dragons wouldn't relax until the threat was completely eliminated.

"Do we ever get to go to Angelino's?" Brooks asked as he pulled a string over the carpet to entertain Marmalade.

Rogan's first impulse was to refuse, wanting to protect his mate at home. One glance at Brooks's face told him sheltering this man completely would not be positive. He forced himself to nod. "How about for lunch tomorrow?"

"Thanks, Rogan. I'd love that. Can Marmalade come?"

The small kitten's complete lack of fear of his dragon needled at Rogan. How could anything so helpless not cringe when confronted with his raw power? Marmalade's bravery matched his mate's. Wherever Brooks went, the orange kitten followed. He'd even gone on patrol flights with the two of them, napping without a shred of uneasiness in a messenger bag slung over Brooks's chest.

"No. Marmalade can't visit the restaurant," Rogan declared.

"But the other mates will want to meet him."

"We'll host a gathering soon to introduce him."

"Oh, good idea. I bet Skye will draw him for me. I'd love to hang a picture in my room," Brooks shared.

"You can ask her tomorrow," Rogan suggested as the fearless kitten stalked toward him. He snarled to scare him, letting the furry tabby see the red flash in his eyes. Marmalade didn't hesitate. He climbed Rogan's pant leg with those needle-sharp kitten claws and curled up on his lap.

"He likes you too. Maybe you have two mates," Brooks suggested with twinkling eyes.

"I do not have a cat for a mate. Felines and dragons are sworn enemies," Rogan growled.

"Are you sure about that? I see a lot of similarities. You both purr very loudly."

Rogan raised his gaze from the soft kitten to his mate, giving him a warning glare. Brooks laughed, completely unfazed by his ferocity just as Marmalade was. Rogan shook his head. His mate didn't need an accomplice to keep him on his toes. Brooks could handle that perfectly well on his own.

"Will Keres join us?" Brooks asked, changing the subject.

"At Angelino's? I doubt it. He's been scarce. He visited Oldrik a few days ago, and no one has seen him since."

"What does Oldrik say?"

"Not much. Something is going on there, and the two of them aren't sharing information with the horde. I don't think Ardon even knows what's happening," Rogan shared.

"That's suspicious."

"It certainly is. Maybe we'll find out more tomorrow over pizza," Rogan suggested as Brooks stood and walked to his side.

"Can I join you two, or is this a private party?" Brooks asked, leaning forward to pet Marmalade.

"Save me, please," Rogan requested and scooped up the cat to pass him over to his mate before lifting Brooks onto his lap. Rogan brushed his mate's bangs out of his face. "We need to get your hair cut again. This lock is completely red. It might be I'm rubbing off on you."

"I like it, Daddy. They say old married people start to look alike after years together."

"Would you like to get married?" Rogan asked, watching his mate's reaction closely.

"I was never married, so I don't speak from experience, but the mate bond is a bigger commitment than a piece of paper and rice thrown in the air."

"It is, but humans like their traditions. If you want to be pelted by rice on the church steps, let me know," Rogan teased.

"I'll keep that in mind," Brooks promised as he rolled his eyes at his Daddy's silliness.

"Let me see your neck, Adventurer."

"It's healed, Daddy."

"Almost." Rogan brushed a fingertip lightly over the faint line and felt his mate shiver in reaction to his touch. Thank goodness Brooks had survived. Rogan would never forget the sight of a knife held at his throat. "You're not to scare me again, Brooks."

"I promise, Daddy. Dragons seem all tough and vicious outside, but inside you guys are marshmallows."

"No telling."

"My lips are sealed."

"How about if you go grab Rogue and we set off on an adventure today? I'm going to pick up a couple of treadmills from a sporting goods store," Rogan shared.

"For lawn art?" Brooks suggested saucily.

"Very funny, Adventurer. The miller has discovered he can use the treads manually to move large containers of grain more easily."

"That makes sense. So, we're going to swoop in and snare a few treadmills for you to carry home?"

"That's what I planned. Why? Want something else?"

"Do you think the sporting goods store might have an old-fashioned crank ice cream maker?" Brooks asked.

"I have one of those," Rogan assured him. "Fancy eating a cold treat?"

"Crap. We'd need ice, wouldn't we?" Brooks slumped in dejection.

"If you take a coat and gloves, we could stop for snow on the top of a mountain."

"I'll find warm clothes."

"Perfect. Go grab those, and I'll unearth the ice cream maker and confiscate a cooler. The cook is making brownies tonight for you. We can have sundaes if you would like," Rogan suggested.

"Now, that's an adventure. I'll go find a coat!"

He smiled as his mate bolted from the room in excitement. Rogan hoped Keres would be successful in his search. No one should be alone.

I wish you good luck, Keres.

The response was faint. *I'll take it. I need all the luck I can get.*

Thank you for reading Rogan: Fated Dragon Daddies 5!

Don't miss future sweet and steamy Daddy stories by Pepper North? Subscribe to my newsletter!

Are you ready for the final story in the Fated Dragon series? Keres: Fated Dragon Daddies 6 is coming soon!

When all hope has evaporated, his search will focus on replacing himself.

Rogan

Sumire has existed in the haze of a mountain shielded by clouds. Always dreaming of the sun, she's never risked basking in its warmth. As the last hope for desperate dragons, being cherished as a fated mate is not this female's destiny.

Keres has lived without a mate for too long. His battle to cling to sanity is coming to an end. Only one choice remains—abandon his need for a Wyvern mate to hunt something more elusive. The clock is ticking as blackness consumes his mind and soul.

Change has come to Wyvern. A centuries-old pact between the founders and their powerful allies could save the inhabitants of the city once again, but only a dragon Daddy can truly guard his mate from harm.

Available for preorder on Amazon now!

Read more from Pepper North

Fated Dragon Daddies

Change is coming to Wyvern.
A centuries-old pact between the founders and their powerful allies could save the inhabitants of the city once again, but only a dragon Daddy can truly guard his mate from harm.

Shadowridge Guardians

Combining the sizzling talents of bestselling authors Pepper North, Kate Oliver, and Becca Jameson, the Shadowridge Guardians are guaranteed to give you a thrill and leave you dreaming of your own throbbing motorcycle joyride.

Are you daring enough to ride with a club of rough, growly, commanding men? The protective Daddies of the Shadowridge Guardians Motorcycle Club will stop at nothing to ensure the safety and protection of everything that belongs to them: their Littles, their club, and their town. Throw in some sassy, naughty, mischievous women who won't hesitate to serve their fair share of attitude even in the face of looming danger, and this brand new MC Romance series is ready to ignite!

Pepper North

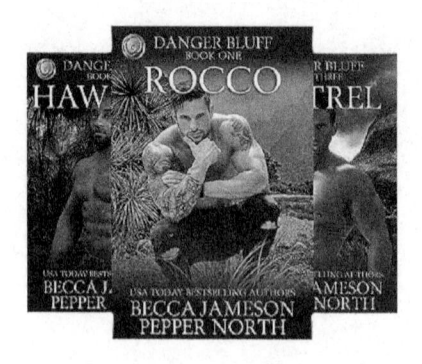

Danger Bluff

Welcome to Danger Bluff where a mysterious billionaire brings together a hand-selected team of men at an abandoned resort in New Zealand. They each owe him a marker. And they all have something in common–a dominant shared code to nurture and protect. They will repay their debts one by one, finding love along the way.

Rogan

A Second Chance For Mr. Right

For some, there is a second chance at having Mr. Right. Coulda, Shoulda, Woulda explores a world of connections that can't exist... until they do. Forbidden love abounds when these Daddy Doms refuse to live with regret and claim the women who own their hearts.

Pepper North

Little Cakes

Welcome to Little Cakes, the bakery that plays Daddy matchmaker! Little Cakes is a sweet and satisfying series, but dare to taste only if you like delicious Daddies, luscious Littles, and guaranteed happily-ever-afters.

Dr. Richards' Littles®

A beloved age play series that features Littles who find their forever Daddies and Mommies. Dr. Richards guides and supports their efforts to keep their Littles happy and healthy.

Note: Zoey; Dr. Richards' Littles® 1 is available FREE on Pepper's website:
4PepperNorth.club

Dr. Richards' Littles®
is a registered trademark of
With A Wink Publishing, LLC.
All rights reserved.

SANCTUM

Pepper North introduces you to an age play community that is isolated from the surrounding world. Here Littles can be Little, and Daddies can care for their Littles and keep them protected from the outside world.

Soldier Daddies

What private mission are these elite soldiers undertaking? They're all searching for their perfect Little girl.

Pepper North

The Keepers

This series from Pepper North is a twist on contemporary age play romances. Here are the stories of humans cared for by specially selected Keepers of an alien race. These are science fiction novels that age play readers will love!

The Magic of Twelve

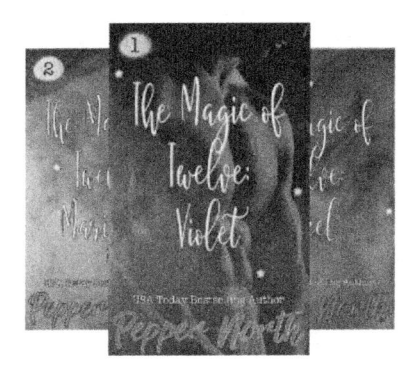

The Magic of Twelve features the stories of twelve women transported on their 22nd birthday to a new life as the droblin (cherished Little one) of a Sorcerer of Bairn. These magic wielders have waited a long time to take complete care of their droblin's needs. They will protect their precious one to their last drop of magic from a growing menace. Each novel is a complete story.

Pepper North

Ever just gone for it? That's what *USA Today* Bestselling Author Pepper North did in 2017 when she posted a book for sale on Amazon without telling anyone. Thanks to her amazing fans, the support of the writing community, Mr. North, and a killer schedule, she has now written more than 180 books! Enjoy contemporary, paranormal, dark, and erotic romances that are both sweet and steamy? Pepper will convert you into one of her loyal readers. What's coming in the future? A Daddypalooza!

Sign up for Pepper North's newsletter

Like Pepper North on Facebook

Join Pepper's Readers' Group for insider information and giveaways!

Follow Pepper everywhere!
Amazon Author Page
BookBub
FaceBook
GoodReads
Instagram
TikToc
Twitter
YouTube
Visit Pepper's website for a current checklist of books!

Printed in Great Britain
by Amazon